The Secret of the Sacred Temple:
Cambodia

The Pursuit of the Ivory Poachers:
Kenya

The Puzzle of the Missing Panda:
China

Peril at the Grand Prix:
Italy

BOOKS 5–8

Elizabeth Singer Hunt
Illustrated by Brian Williamson

WEINSTEIN
BOOKS

Printed in the United States of America.

Cataloging-in-Publication data for this book is available
from the Library of Congress.

ISBN: 978-1-60286-326-2 (print)

Published by Weinstein Books
A member of the Perseus Books Group
www.weinsteinbooks.com

Weinstein Books are available at special discounts
for bulk purchases in the U.S. by corporations,
institutions and other organizations. For more
information, please contact the
Special Markets Department at
the Perseus Books Group,
2300 Chestnut Street, Suite 200,
Philadelphia, PA 19103,
call (800) 810-4145, ext. 5000, or
e-mail special.markets@perseusbooks.com.

First edition

10 9 8 7 6 5 4 3 2 1

The Secret of the
Sacred Temple:
CAMBODIA

BOOK (5)

Join Agent Jack Stalwart on his Adventures:

The Secret of the Sacred Temple: CAMBODIA

Elizabeth Singer Hunt

Illustrated by Brian Williamson

WEINSTEIN BOOKS

For the people of Southeast Asia,
my "home away from home"

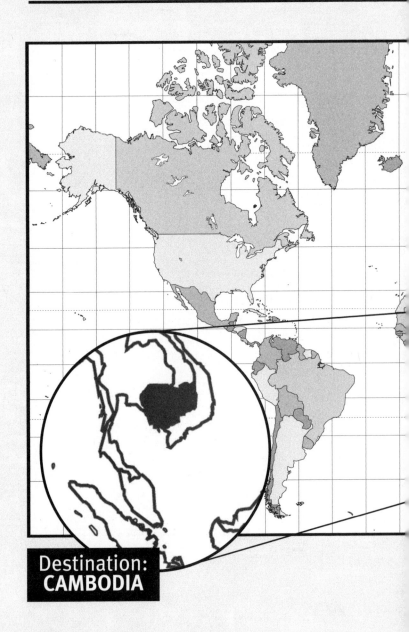

Destination:
CAMBODIA

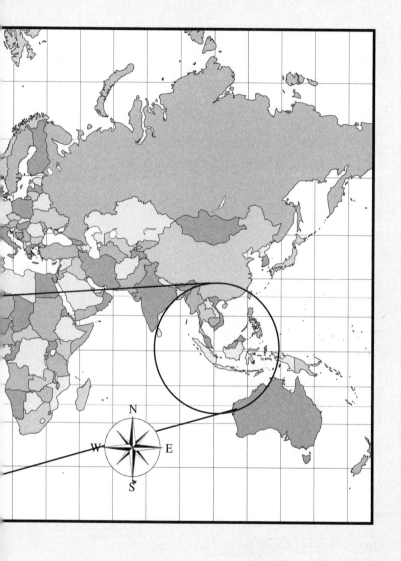

My name is Jack Stalwart. My older brother,

Max, was a secret agent for you, until he

disappeared on one of your missions. Now I

want to be a secret agent, too. If you choose

me, I will be an excellent secret agent and get

rid of evil villains, just like my brother did.

Sincerely,

Jack Stalwart

THINGS YOU'LL FIND IN EVERY BOOK

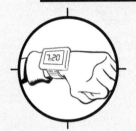

Watch Phone: The only gadget Jack wears all the time, even when he's not on official business. His Watch Phone is the central gadget that makes most others work. There are lots of important features, most importantly the C button, which reveals the code of the day—necessary to unlock Jack's Secret Agent Book Bag. There are buttons on both sides, one of which ejects his life-saving Melting Ink Pen. Beyond these functions, it also works as a phone and, of course, gives Jack the time of day.

Global Protection Force (GPF): The GPF is the organization Jack works for. It's a worldwide force of young secret agents whose aim is to protect the world's people, places, and possessions. No one knows exactly where its main offices are located (all correspondence and gadgets for repair are sent to a special PO Box, and training is held at various locations around the world), but Jack thinks it's somewhere cold, like the Arctic Circle.

Whizzy: Jack's magical miniature globe. Almost every night at precisely 7:30 PM, the GPF uses Whizzy to send Jack the identity of the country that he must travel to. Whizzy can't talk, but he can cough up messages. Jack's parents don't know Whizzy is anything more than a normal globe.

The Magic Map: The magical map hanging on Jack's bedroom wall. Unlike most maps, the GPF's map is made of a mysterious wood. Once Jack inserts the country piece from Whizzy, the map swallows Jack whole and sends him away on his missions. When he returns, he arrives precisely one minute after he left.

Secret Agent Book Bag: The Book Bag that Jack wears on every adventure. Licensed only to GPF secret agents, it contains top-secret gadgets necessary to foil bad guys and escape certain death. To activate the bag before each mission, Jack must punch in a secret code given to him by his Watch Phone. Once he's away, all he has to do is place his finger on the zipper, which identifies him as the owner of the bag and it immediately opens.

THE STALWART FAMILY

Jack's dad, John

He moved the family to England when Jack was two, in order to take a job with an aerospace company. As far as Jack knows, his dad designs and manufactures airplane parts. Jack's dad thinks he is an ordinary boy and that his other son, Max, attends a school in Switzerland. Jack's dad is American and his mum is British, which makes Jack a bit of both.

Jack's mum, Corinne

One of the greatest mums as far as Jack is concerned. When she and her husband received a letter from a posh school in Switzerland inviting Max to attend, they were overjoyed. Since Max left six months ago, they have received numerous notes in Max's handwriting telling them he's OK. Little do they know it's all a lie and that it's the GPF sending those letters.

Jack's older brother, Max

Two years ago, at the age of nine, Max joined the GPF. Max used to tell Jack about his adventures and show him how to work his secret-agent gadgets. When the family received a letter inviting Max to attend a school in Europe, Jack figured it was to do with the GPF. Max told him he was right, but that he couldn't tell Jack anything about why he was going away.

Nine-year-old Jack Stalwart

Four months ago, Jack received an anonymous note saying: "Your brother is in danger. Only you can save him." As soon as he could, Jack applied to be a secret agent, too. Since that time, he's battled some of the world's most dangerous villains and hopes some day in his travels to find and rescue his brother, Max.

DESTINATION:
Cambodia

The temple of Angkor Wat was built by a king called Suryavarman II (pronounced *Surrey-ya-varmin*) between 1113 and 1150.

☐

The word Angkor means "city."

☐

The word Wat means "temple."

☐

The official language of Cambodia is Khmer (pronounced *Ka-mare*).

☐

The main religion in Cambodia is Buddhism.

Cambodia is located in Southeast Asia.

☐

The capital city of Cambodia is Phnom Penh (pronounced *Pe-nom Pen*).

☐

Fourteen million people live in Cambodia.

☐

The largest river in Southeast Asia, the Mekong, flows through Cambodia.

SECRET AGENT PHRASEBOOK FOR CAMBODIA

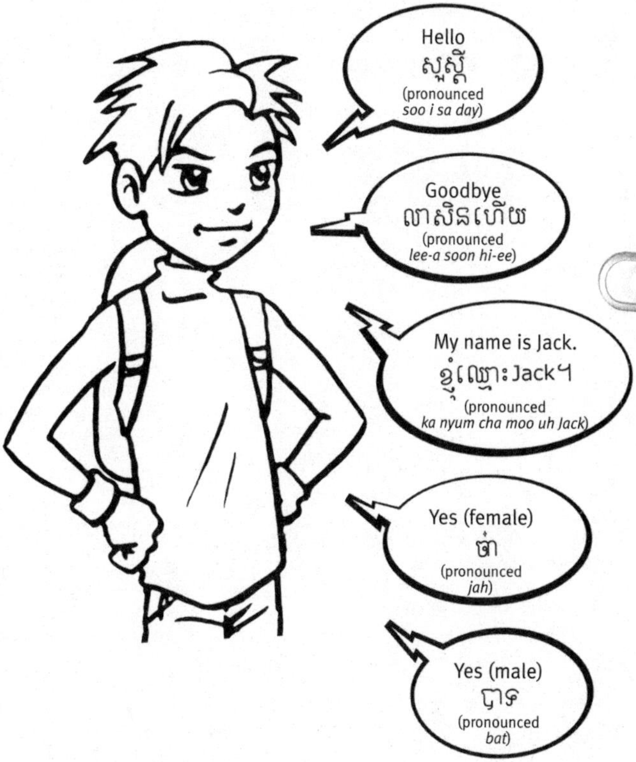

Angkor

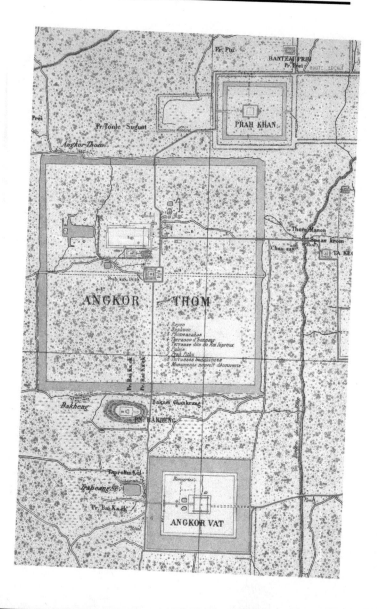

Cambodia

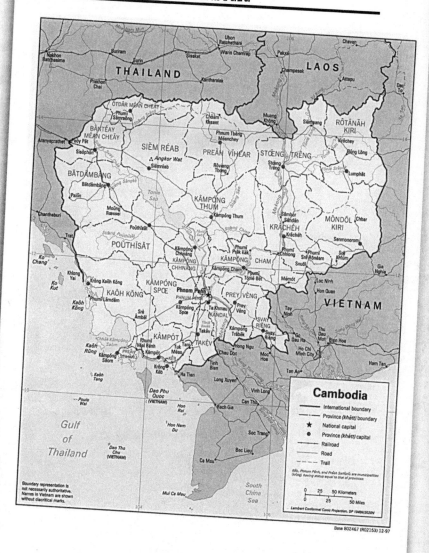

Cambodia

- ——— International boundary
- ‑‑‑ Province *(khétt)* boundary
- ★ National capital
- ● Province *(khétt)* capital
- ——— Railroad
- ——— Road
- ‑‑‑ Trail

Kêb, Phnum Pénh, and Preâh Seihânŭ are municipalities (krŏng) having status equal to that of provinces.

```
0    25    50 Kilometers
0    25    50 Miles
```

Lambert Conformal Conic Projection, SP 104N/2020N

Boundary representation is
not necessarily authoritative.
Names in Vietnam are shown
without diacritical marks.

Base 802467 (R02153) 12-97

SECRET AGENT GADGET INSTRUCTION MANUAL

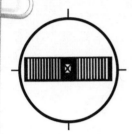 **Transponder:** Ideal for tracking a friend or an evil villain. Just place this small, sticky plastic piece on someone (or something) and activate the *T* button on your Watch Phone. Instantly, the location of the Transponder will appear.

 **Mine Alert:** Imbedded into every standard-issue secret-agent shoe. Just flick the "alert" switch on the outside of your shoe and wait for a green light to come out of the tip. As soon as you start to move, the Mine Alert lasers sweep the territory ahead, sending vibrations through your shoe if you're about to step on a bomb.

Electrolyte Dust:

Whenever you've been knocked senseless by your opponent or feel dehydrated, just peel open the orange pack and sprinkle the dust on your tongue. It will instantly revive you and restore important salts to your body, making you feel refreshed.

Body-Count Tracker:

An excellent hand-held device for mapping out a location before you've even entered it. The Body-Count Tracker will show you where the walls, doors, windows, and ceilings are located in every room and whether there are any people inside. It can also tell you whether they are alive or dead, a useful tool for any secret agent entering the unknown.

Chapter 1:
The Annoying One

"And then you'll never guess what happened," gushed Lily, Jack's eleven-year-old cousin. She was visiting Jack's family from Devon, where Jack's Aunt Emma, Lily's mum, lived. "My friend Luke stood in front of the class to read his essay and didn't even know that his shirttail was stuck in the zipper of his trousers! Isn't that embarrassing?"

The whole family—Jack, his dad, his mum and Lily—were sitting around the dinner table finishing a delicious fish-and-chip supper. If the story had

1

been told by anyone else, Jack would have found it funny. But because it was told by his annoying cousin, he just rolled his eyes and looked at his mum.

"That's a nice story, Lily," said Jack's mum to Lily. "Did anything exciting happen to you today?" she asked, turning her attention to Jack.

Just as Jack was about to tell his family about how he had scored the winning goal in today's football match, he spied the clock hanging on the wall above his mother's head. It read 7:28 PM. He looked back at his mum and smiled before he leaped from his chair and headed for the kitchen door.

"Lots of stuff, Mum," said Jack, "but it'll have to wait until tomorrow. I've got math homework to do!" He left the kitchen and quickly climbed the stairs to his bedroom.

Jack's dad, who had up until now listened silently to the conversation at the table, said proudly, "It's wonderful that Jack has taken such an interest in math."

As Jack began to open his bedroom door, he could hear his cousin still talking downstairs. "Guess what happened to my friend Frieda McCauley today?" she squealed excitedly to her aunt and uncle.

"Someone stole a hairbrush out of her bag!"

Poor Mum and Dad, Jack thought, shaking his head. Glad I have some math homework. He smiled to himself as he opened the door and stepped into his top-secret bedroom.

Chapter 2:
The Secret

Jack entered the room, hung his KEEP OUT
sign on the doorknob and closed the
door behind him. There was always the
possibility that a family member would
walk in and discover something Jack
didn't want them to see—like Whizzy
telling him about his next mission, or Jack
surveying his latest hi-tech gadgets.

Jack was a secret agent for the Global
Protection Force. The Global Protection
Force, or GPF, sent Jack around the globe
in order to protect the world's most
precious people, places, and things.

Protect that which cannot protect itself was the motto of the Global Protection Force. The organization was started in 1947 by a man named Ronald Barter who decided he'd had enough of crooks trying to destroy things that mattered in the world. Things like beautiful pieces of art, endangered animals, famous buildings, or even famous people who were trying to do something positive. When he died in 1962 (in mysterious circumstances), his son Gerald took over and made the GPF one of the leading worldwide forces against crime.

Jack joined the GPF after his older brother, Max, disappeared. Although no one else in his family knew that Max was a secret agent for the GPF, Jack did. That was because Max had told him.

Max used to show Jack his secret-agent gadgets and explain how they worked as he told him stories about using each one on his missions. Jack looked forward to those times with Max so he could hear all about the adventures. Although lots of brothers their age didn't get along, Jack and Max got along well. They were more like best friends.

Then Max was sent by the GPF to a supposed school in Switzerland.

When Jack received the anonymous note telling him his brother was in danger, he quickly signed up to join the GPF and dedicated his life to finding Max. As soon as he was on the "inside," he asked the GPF about Max's whereabouts, but the GPF wouldn't tell Jack a thing. Everyone denied any involvement in Max's disappearance and immediately sealed Max's files.

Even so, Jack always hoped that one of his missions would lead to some information about Max. Who knows? thought Jack that evening, maybe this mission will be the one.

Chapter 3:
The Foreign Land

Suddenly, there was a buzzing sound
from the side of Jack's bed. Whizzy, Jack's
magical miniature globe, was spinning
hard to try to get Jack's
attention and to build
up enough speed to
hurl the jigsaw piece
inside him out onto
the floor.

"Ahem!" Whizzy
coughed. A jigsaw
piece flew out of
his mouth so fast

that it hit the wall opposite and bounced back onto the floor near Jack's desk.

Jack walked over and picked up the piece. Looking at it, he had no idea what country it could be. There was nothing distinctive about it. No long bits. No short bits. Just a rounded country that didn't look like anywhere in particular.

Jack carried the piece over to his wall where there was an amazing map of the world, with every single country carved into it. One morning, not long after he was sworn in at the GPF, Jack woke up and found the map there. Now, how was he going to explain *this* to his parents, he thought. In the end, he just shrugged and said that it was a prize from one of his teachers.

He picked up the piece and started to move it over the map. He was looking for that "perfect fit," where the jigsaw piece slotted neatly into a country on the wall.

As Jack's hand stroked the map, his eyes scanned the continents. Not America, not Africa, not Europe. What about Asia? He glanced at India (which was too big) and started going over Burma and Thailand. Just past Thailand, Jack looked at the wall and noticed something. The shape of the jigsaw piece and the shape of the country to the southeast of Thailand matched. He pushed the piece onto the wall and it snapped in. The name CAMBODIA flashed on the wall once and then disappeared.

"Cambodia?" said Jack, completely surprised. As far as he knew, it was now a peaceful country without much need for the likes of the GPF.

Just as Jack was trying to remember everything he'd learned about the country in his GPF training, a pink light inside Cambodia started to glow. He didn't have much time.

Jack hurried across his room and reached under his bed. He grabbed his Secret Agent Book Bag then pushed the C button on his Watch Phone. The word T-E-M-P-L-E appeared on the mini-screen. He punched the letters into the lock on his Book Bag and it immediately opened.

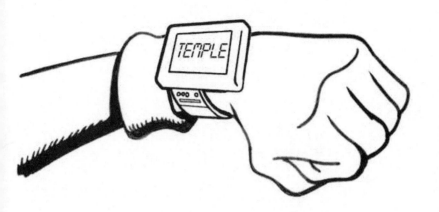

Jack quickly checked that all the essential gadgets were inside. The old standbys— the Magic Key Maker, the Expand-A-Rope, and the Net Tosser—were there, along with new tools like the Depth Barometer, the Body-Count Tracker, and the Voice-Recognition Passport.

He locked his Book Bag, hurried over to the wall and stood before it just as the pink light grew to fill his entire room. When he knew the time was right, he yelled, "Off to Cambodia!" The pink light flickered and burst, swallowing Jack into his Magic Map.

Chapter 4:
The Drop-Off

The next thing Jack knew he was falling head first out of the sky towards the ground below. He was traveling so fast that he could feel the skin on his face being pushed backwards towards his ears.

Directly below him he could see a massive, ancient temple surrounded by water and hidden in the jungle. The temple looked beautiful, like something out of an *Indiana Jones* or *Tomb Raider* movie. But this wasn't the time to admire a beautiful work of architecture. Not when he was about to be splattered all over it.

Just need to reach a bit further, he told himself as he strained to find the small cord attached to his Secret Agent Book Bag. He knew that if he pulled the string, it would release a hidden parachute from his bag, which would carry him gently to the ground.

SNAP! Jack pulled the cord. Nothing happened. He lifted his hand in front of his face, his eyes widening when he saw the small bit of the string he was holding. Panic filled his body as he realized the parachute was broken.

Jack was now falling fast. Near the monument, he could see a gathering of people. They had noticed him hurtling towards the ground without a parachute and were crowding together, anxious to see what would happen.

Quickly, he tucked his knees close to his chest and reached for his left shoe.

He twisted open the heel of the shoe and grabbed a small disc from inside. This was The Dome, a small, round disc with a highly elastic material inside, normally used by secret agents as an expandable bag. Since he didn't have a parachute, he had no choice but to try The Dome instead. He somersaulted in the air so that his feet were facing the ground and lifted the disc high above his head, using both hands. As he continued to fall, the elastic material began to expand like a balloon. It took all Jack's strength to hold onto it, but The Dome was acting just like a normal parachute, helping to slow down his descent.

He was only about thirty feet from the ground when, without warning, the elastic material inside The Dome burst. Jack dropped straight towards the ground. Luckily for him, it wasn't the ground, but

the water near the monument that broke
his fall.

SPLASH!

Jack landed feet first in the dirty, murky
water. When his head came up again,
he gasped for air. The crowd that had
gathered started to shout and cheer.
It wasn't everyday that someone fell out

of the sky without a parachute and lived to tell the tale.

As Jack looked at the crowd, a girl about his own age bent down.

"You must be Jack," she said. "Here, let me help you out," she offered, extending her hand.

Jack paused for a second, confused as to how this young girl knew who he was. He noticed that she was wearing a

necklace with a medallion on it. On the medallion was an image of a man with four hands. Jack reached up towards the girl and put his hand in hers.

When she had pulled Jack out of the water and onto the walkway, she looked at him. "My name is Kate," she said. "Nice of you to drop in," she added. A smile spread across her face. "I've been waiting for you."

Chapter 5:
The Mission

"What? You're my contact?" he asked, wiping the water off his face. "I don't understand. Normally," he added, "I'd be meeting with an adult."

"Well, I'm sorry to disappoint you," Kate said, wrinkling her mouth at Jack, "but I am the one who called the GPF. My mum told me to call them if anything happened. And, well"—she paused, her voice breaking slightly—"since it has, I thought I should call right away."

"What do you mean?" he asked. "What's happened?"

In the split second it took before she answered the question, Jack took a proper look at Kate. Nice green eyes. Nice smile. Nice curly, brown hair. Plus, she wasn't loud like his cousin Lily. Instead, she had a soft-sounding voice. Loud girls were always annoying as far as Jack was concerned.

"My mum's been kidnapped," Kate said. The statement snapped Jack out of his private thoughts.

"Kidnapped?" he asked. "When? Where? Why?"

"Yesterday," said Kate. "I came home from school and the house was a mess. I waited for hours for my mum to come home from work at the temple but she never did."

"What do you mean 'the temple'?" asked Jack. "Which one was she working on?"

"You know, the ancient temple of Angkor

Wat," she said. "You nearly fell on it before landing in the water."

Jack looked at the enormous temple behind him. It had five pointed towers, the middle one of which was the tallest. The temple was huge. It was awe-inspiring.

"The temple of Angkor Wat was one of

many temples built in the ancient city of Angkor," Kate explained. "The city was built by the Khmer people of Cambodia about a thousand years ago. At that time, the Khmers were very powerful and ruled much of Southeast Asia." Kate paused and then carried on. "In order to pray to their gods and bury their kings, they built a series of temples, one of which was Angkor Wat. Then, in the fifteenth century, the Thai people invaded from across the border in Thailand, and the Khmers fled, leaving the temples behind."

"Who looked after the temples then?" asked Jack.

"Over the years," answered Kate, "the jungles grew over them and hid them completely. They weren't discovered again until the nineteenth century. Since that time," she added, "archaeologists have been trying to protect them. The weather here is harsh and people try to steal artifacts from the temples, as they're worth a lot of money."

"So why are you and your mum here?" asked Jack.

"My mum is one of the chief archaeologists watching over the temple of Angkor Wat," said Kate proudly. "We moved here a few months ago."

"But why would someone want to kidnap your mum?" asked Jack. "It sounds as if she was trying to help."

"I don't know," said Kate, shrugging her shoulders and looking down at the walkway. "That's why I contacted the GPF. I don't think I can find my mum without your help."

Jack thought about what Kate was saying. Although this seemed like the straightforward kidnapping of an important person, he couldn't help but feel that there was something more sinister going on. He needed more facts.

"Where was your mother last seen?" asked Jack.

"At home," said Kate. "I'll take you there."

"Great," said Jack, following Kate as she set off along the walkway.

Chapter 6:
The Clue

When they arrived at Kate's house,
escaping the humid weather outside,
Jack was surprised at the terrible state it
was in. The house was an absolute mess.
Tables had been turned upside down.
Pictures had been ripped from the walls.
Curtains had been shredded to bits.
Pretty much everything that had been
standing on its own legs was now
overturned on the cold, stone floor.

Quickly, Jack walked around the house,
making sure it was safe and that there
was no one else inside. He came back

to Kate, who was standing in the living room.

Jack took a few minutes to think. He wondered whether the mess was because of a struggle between Kate's mum and her captors, or if it was because someone was looking for something they thought Kate's mum had.

"When I came home from school," explained Kate, "the house was like this and my mum was missing. Now do you see why I called the GPF?"

"Sure do," said Jack, still amazed at the sight of Kate's house.

"What should we do?" asked Kate. "How are we going to find my mum? The jungle around the temples is huge—she could be anywhere by now."

Jack inspected the room more carefully. If there had been a struggle between Kate's mum and her captors, the house wouldn't have looked this bad. No, thought Jack, this was definitely the result of someone looking for something. But what?

"Did your mum keep anything valuable in the house, like one of those artifacts from the temples?" asked Jack.

"No," said Kate. "Mum didn't take anything from the temples."

Jack's eyes were roaming around the room, looking for clues that might lead them in the right direction. He lifted up the upside-down tables and chairs and looked at the darker patches on the walls where the pictures had hung. As far as Jack could tell, there weren't any false walls or secret compartments in the house where Kate's mum could have hidden something.

Jack bent down to check under the sofa. As he was looking, he spied a small rectangular box. He grabbed it and brought it out into the light of the room. He took a closer look.

"That's my mum's voice recorder," said Kate.

"A voice recorder?" said Jack curiously.

"You know," explained Kate, "a tape recorder. My mum took it wherever she went so that she could record her observations and then play them back later in the day."

Jack looked inside the small cassette window. The tape seemed to be at the end of Side A. Jack rewound it and pushed the "play" button. He turned up the volume and listened.

A frightened female voice began to speak: "To whomever finds this tape, this is Rachel Newington, chief archaeologist

and protector of the temple of Angkor Wat. At any moment, the forces of darkness will descend, searching for the map of the central well. The map must be sent away before they acquire it. Find my daughter and—"

CRASH! There was the sound of breaking glass.

"Oh, my God," the woman whispered into the recorder, "they're here!"

SLAM! A door hit the wall as it was flung open. Then there was the sound of the voice recorder being dropped and kicked across the floor.

"Hello, Rachel," said a man's voice, which grew louder as he walked further into the room. "So nice to see you again."

"Get out of my house!" she shouted. "Get out of Cambodia!"

"Come now, Rachel," said the man. "There's no need to be difficult. I'm sure you know why we're here. Just hand it over and all will be well."

"I'll never give you the map!" she screamed. "You'll have to kill me first!"

The man laughed nastily. "That part's negotiable, my dear," he said. "Let's make this easy. Hand over the map."

"Never!" she screamed.

"Chai!" shouted the man. There was the sound of someone else walking into the room. "Why don't you escort Rachel to the Temple of the Trees and we'll see whether we can't force the location of the map out of her?"

There were muffled sounds of Kate's mum being dragged away. Then the door closed.

CRASH! It sounded as though furniture was being thrown around.

SCREECH! Chairs were slid across the floor. Someone was still there.

"Where is it? Where is it, you dreadful

woman?" the man demanded furiously. "I'll find it, Rachel," he cursed, "whatever it takes!"

There was the sound of the man leaving the room and slamming the door behind him, then silence.

Chapter 7:
The Surprise

Jack turned off the tape recorder and looked at Kate. Tears were welling up in her eyes.

"Don't worry, Kate," he said, trying to make her feel better. "I'll find your mum. I promise."

Kate sniffed the tears away. "I know," she said. "I trust you. My mum said that if you were anything like your brother you'd be a terrific secret agent."

Jack stood there, stunned into temporary silence.

"What do you mean, my brother?" he

said, almost too shocked to register what she had actually said. "How do you know my brother?" he asked, his voice starting to quiver.

"Well, I don't know him personally," Kate said, "but my mum met him when she was working in Egypt. There were some problems on her project and she had to call the GPF. Your brother was the agent assigned to the case."

"Egypt?" asked Jack. He had no idea his brother had been assigned to a project in Egypt. "What else do you know?" he went on frantically. "What do you mean there were problems? What kind of project was she working on? You have to tell me everything!"

"But I don't know any more," said Kate. "That's all I know. My mum said she'd heard that you'd become a secret agent, too, and that I should call you if anything happened. She trusted your brother, so I guess she decided to trust you, too."

Jack felt as if he were going to faint. He couldn't believe that he was sitting in the middle of this girl's house in the Cambodian jungle, hearing about his brother Max, who'd been missing for four months. He had to find Kate's mum—not just because that was his assignment, but also because she must be able to tell him more about Max's disappearance.

"Right," said Jack, with a new sense of urgency. "We need to find your mum. The man on the tape mentioned the 'Temple of the Trees.' Any idea which of the temples that could be?"

"Well," said Kate, "a lot of the temples have trees around them, but there's only one that has trees inside it. They're growing through the walls, in fact," she added. "And that's the Temple of Ta Phrom."

Chapter 8:
The Jungle

"Let's get going," said Jack, tightening the straps on his Book Bag.

"It's too far to walk," said Kate, "we'll have to take the bikes."

Jack and Kate hurried outside and grabbed two bicycles off the rack in front of Kate's house. Before setting off, Jack grabbed Kate's arm and pulled her back.

"Wait," he said, handing her a small piece of plastic. "Put this in your shoe."

"What is it?" she asked.

"It's a Transponder," said Jack. "You

know, so I can find you in case you get lost or something."

"Yeah, right," said Kate. "Like I'm going to get lost. I live here, remember. I know this place like the back of my hand! If anyone's going to get lost, it's you!"

"Well, it would make me feel better if you had it," said Jack. He knew that his Watch Phone had a tracking device linked to the Transponder, so if she did get lost, he'd be able to find her.

"OK. OK," she said as she reluctantly placed the Transponder in her shoe.

Kate pushed off and pedaled ahead, guiding Jack down a narrow dirt path and onto a road that led deep into the jungle. The longer they rode, the more difficult it was to see. The sun was setting fast and the road they were cycling on was shrouded by tall, leafy trees. Squinting, Jack could just about see Kate pedaling ahead and a family of fruit bats swarming above her.

After about ten minutes, Kate began to slow down. She pulled over to the side of the road and pushed her bike into the trees. Jack did the same and stood next

to Kate. They had already agreed to park the bikes away from the temple and approach on foot.

"How far is it from here?" he asked.

"About a minute's walk," she said, pointing between the trees.

Jack stepped into the forest, but Kate grabbed his hand, pulling him back.

"Wait!" she said. "You need to be careful. There are lots of land mines in the ground. They were left here during a civil war years ago and some haven't been

detonated yet. I'd hate for you to be blown up before we find my mum," she added, smiling. Jack couldn't tell if she was joking or not.

In case she wasn't, Jack bent down towards his shoes and activated the Mine Alert. Instantly, two long green lights shot out of the tips of his shoes and began moving from side to side, like windshield wipers, scanning the ground.

"Cool," she said, looking down at Jack's feet.

"Yeah," said Jack, pleased that his gadget had impressed her. "These will tell us if there are any land mines ahead. Stick close," he added, "and step in exactly the same spots as I do."

"You got it," said Kate, standing close behind him. Then they both headed off into the jungle, carefully winding their way towards the Temple of the Trees.

Chapter 9:
The Temple of
the Trees

As the forest began to clear, Jack could
see the Temple of Ta Phrom in the
distance. It was an eerie site, the kind of
haunted-looking place that people pay
good money to try to recreate for
Halloween at home.

It had enormous silvery trees growing
inside and through its walls. Their large
roots slithered over the stone like the
tentacles of a giant octopus. The roots
were slowly prying the temple apart, one
piece at a time. Large white patches of

lichen covered its walls, sucking whatever nutrients it could find in the stone. Jack thought he could hear the temple moaning. He gulped and looked out of the corner of his eye at Kate. He was more than just a little bit nervous, but he tried not to show it.

Jack took a deep breath and approached the temple's entrance. He unzipped his Book Bag and took out his Body-Count Tracker—a hand-held device that could tell you how many people were inside a building before you even entered it. It could also tell you whether they were alive or dead: a green figure meant alive, a red one dead. Jack switched it on and focused it at the door of the temple so it could scan the area.

He stared at the screen. A floor plan of the temple appeared, showing him the exact layout. Jack moved the arrow

buttons up and down, trawling through the image. From what he could tell, there were three people inside. Two green figures were standing together in one room, while another green body was alone in a different area. If Kate's mum was the body by itself that meant she was still alive!

"That must be your mum," said Jack, pointing to the single green figure.

He walked ahead, using the Body-Count Tracker as a map of the temple. They stepped into the main entrance area and through an open courtyard. Jack looked above him at the sky. Thankfully, the moon was almost full, providing them with just the right amount of light to navigate the temple walls. Above them, he could hear the call of bats.

Facing them was a large square building. Quietly, they walked around the corner and to its left. In the moonlight, Jack could see a wall of carved dancers. They looked as though they were being strangled by the trees, whose finer roots had woven themselves tightly around their necks. Hopefully it wasn't a sign of things to come.

Jack looked again at the Body-Count Tracker. Up to the left was another building. This was where the lone figure was located. The other two people were still on the opposite side of the temple. Quickly, Jack and Kate passed underneath a stone lintel and into the other building. Sitting on the floor, bound and gagged next to a small candle, was Kate's mum.

"Mum!" exclaimed Kate in a loud whisper as she raced over to her mother and hugged her. She quickly untied the gag that was around her mother's mouth.

"Kate!" said her mum, gasping for air. "You need to leave right now! Your life will be in danger if they see you!"

"There's no way I'm leaving without you, Mum," said Kate.

"There's no time!" said Kate's mum, her eyes pleading with her daughter. "You have to go without me. You have the map of the central well!"

"What do you mean I have the map?" said Kate, looking at her mum in disbelief. "You didn't give me any map!"

Kate's mum looked at her and then at the necklace around Kate's neck; the one with the image of the man with four hands. Kate looked down at the necklace, too.

She lifted the medallion up and turned it over. On the back there was an inscription written in a language Kate had never seen before. She looked questioningly at her mum.

"When I became chief archaeologist of the temple," her mother explained quickly, "I was entrusted with this necklace. On the back of the medallion is an ancient inscription that tells the exact location of the central well within the Temple of Angkor Wat. Deep inside the central well is the sacred treasure of the god-king. No one knows what the treasure looks like. Not only is it priceless, it's a source of power to whomever possesses it."

"But how could anyone read what's on the back?" asked Kate, staring at the funny writings on the medallion.

"Only a few people in the world know how to decipher that language," answered

Kate's mum. "And, unfortunately, the man who is after it is one of them."

"Yes, that's right," said a male voice from behind. Jack spun around as two men walked into the room. Jack recognized the voice of the man who was speaking. It was the one from the voice recorder. His companion was a Thai man dressed in silk pantaloon trousers.

"You've saved me a lot of trouble," the man continued, grinning from ear to ear. Jack was temporarily stunned by his smile—the top four teeth in the man's

mouth were not made of enamel, but of pure gold.

"How stupid of you, Rachel," he said, looking at Kate's mum, "to give something so valuable to such a young girl."

"Shut up!" Kate shouted at the man. "You'll never get the map from me!" she said, clutching the necklace in her hands.

"You sound just like your mother," he said, laughing. His gold teeth were shining in the candlelight. "Has anyone ever told you that you look just like her?" He walked over to Kate and stroked her cheek.

"Don't you touch her!" said Jack as he lunged for the man.

But within an instant the man had tossed some powder at Jack that blinded him and instantly made him feel sick. His throat started to swell, making it hard for him to breathe. He coughed and collapsed on the floor, feeling as if he was about to pass out. As Jack slipped in

and out of consciousness, he could hear Kate's voice. It sounded as though it was very far away.

"Jack!" she screamed. "Wake up!"

Then, with Kate's voice sounding even more distant, Jack fell into a deep sleep.

Chapter 10:
The Turning Point

When Jack woke up, it was daytime and he was by himself. There was no Kate and no Kate's mum. Luckily the crooks hadn't taken his Book Bag. Reaching inside and grabbing a small orange packet, Jack opened it and sprinkled the Electrolyte Dust onto his tongue. Instantly, he began to feel better. He sat for a moment and tried to make sense of things while he looked at the light pouring through the temple windows.

He reached into his back pocket and pulled out Kate's mum's voice recorder.

He rewound it and pushed the play button again.

". . . this is Rachel Newington, chief archaeologist and protector of the Temple of Angkor Wat. At any moment, the forces of darkness will descend, searching for the map of the central well. The map must be sent away before they acquire it. Find my daughter and—"

Now the message made sense. As far as Jack could tell, the man with the gold teeth had been looking for the map to the central well, and thought that Kate's mum had it. That was, of course, until Jack and Kate showed up at the temple with Kate wearing it around her neck. Goodness only knew what the man was going to do to Kate now. Jack was starting to feel sick again. He'd really messed things up this time. He closed his eyes and wondered how on earth he was going to find Kate.

With his eyes closed, Jack became aware of a noise in the distance. The noise was growing louder by the second.

BLEEP! BLEEP! BLEEP! It was coming from Jack's Watch Phone. He looked down at the screen.

Of course! thought Jack. At last something was going right. The noise was Kate's Transponder, which he'd temporarily forgotten about.

Quickly Jack punched the T button on his Watch Phone. The words ANGKOR WAT, CAMBODIA flashed across the screen and with it a tiny map of where it was located. The man with the gold teeth must have taken Kate and her mum along with him to the Temple of Angkor Wat, to find the sacred treasure.

"I'm coming, Kate," Jack said out loud as he picked himself up off the floor and raced out of the Temple of the Trees. He'd already been knocked out for hours. There was no time to waste.

Chapter 11:
The Path to
Angkor Wat

Jack found one of the bikes that he and Kate had left in the jungle and pedaled it as quickly as he could down the dirt road towards Angkor Wat.

As he approached the temple, he began to slow down. He surveyed the outside of the massive monument. Angkor Wat was surrounded by a moat filled with water, the one that he had landed in yesterday. Just inside the moat were high stone walls that guarded the ancient temple within. The only way in and out was on the main walkway where he had first met Kate during his free-fall arrival in Cambodia.

Since Angkor Wat was one of the first temples to be restored by the archae-ologists, it had become something of a tourist attraction, with people walking in and out of its walls at all times of the day.

Unfortunately for Jack, that meant extra security precautions. Not only did he have to save Kate and her mum and protect the sacred treasure, but he also had to make sure that no tourists were harmed in the process.

Jack pedaled around the moat and approached the temple from the grand walkway. He hurried along, glancing at the people around him. Crowds were the perfect place for people to hide. He climbed the steps and passed through the first of two doors into the ancient temple grounds. Kate and her mum were nowhere to be seen.

Breathing heavily, he raced through the second door and into a bigger courtyard. He looked to the left, and then to the right. All he could see was tourists milling around. A group of people were taking photos of the strange carvings that lined the covered walkways along the perimeter.

He looked at his Watch Phone and

noted the location of Kate's Transponder. By the look of it, Jack was standing right next to her! But where was she?

It was faint, thought Jack, but he could have sworn he heard a girl scream. He looked at the tourists, who continued taking photos. Another tour group passed by. Jack heard it again. No one in the temple besides Jack seemed to notice it. Maybe that powder had done something to his head and he was imagining things.

Jack looked ahead of him. In the middle of the courtyard was the fifth of the five towers, at the top of which was a small room. The only way up to the room was to climb the incredibly steep stairs, and each one was as high as Jack's legs were long.

"Jack!" It was the girl's voice again. It was Kate's and it was coming from inside the tower. He leaped up onto the first step. Using his hands and knees, he scrambled to the top of the steps and reached the entrance to the tower. Facing him was a sign that read: SANCTUARY CLOSED FOR REPAIRS.

"Yeah, right," said Jack as he hurried past the sign and into the tower.

He found himself standing in the middle of a small, square room with carvings of ancient people all around him.

"Help me!" screamed Kate. He could

hear her clearly now. But where was she? The echo in her voice made it sound as if she were at the bottom of a great cavern.

"Kate!" said Jack, scanning the room to try to find her. "Where are you?"

"I'm down here!" she shouted. "I'm in the central well!"

Jack ran to the middle of the room, stopping suddenly when he found himself teetering on the edge of a deep hole. He looked down into the hole, but couldn't see a thing. It was completely black. Kate must be scared to death down there.

"Hold on!" he shouted to her. "I'll get you out of there!"

Jack yanked open his Secret Agent Book Bag and pulled out his Depth Barometer, which was a tiny round piece of plastic. Once Jack dropped it down the hole, it would feed back to his Watch Phone the exact depth of the well, which

would tell him how much rope he needed to rescue Kate.

He tossed the Depth Barometer down the hole and waited, looking at his Watch Phone. A depth of seventy-five feet flashed on the screen on his wrist. He  pulled his Expand-A-Rope out of his Book Bag and programmed it to grow to seventy-five feet in length. Then he tied one end of the rope around his waist and threw the other end down to Kate.

"I'm throwing you a rope!" he yelled. The rope grew to precisely seventy-five feet and fell straight into Kate's lap at the bottom of the hole.

"Got it!" she yelled back.

"Right!" shouted Jack. "Hold on!" He

braced himself and then programmed the rope to pull her gently upwards.

Jack peered down the entire time, waiting for Kate's face to appear in the darkness. When it did, he was overjoyed.

"Jack!" she screamed excitedly as she climbed out of the well and threw her arms around his neck. "I knew you'd find me! But something terrible has happened! My mum," she added frantically. "They've taken her and the treasure, too!"

"What do you mean?" asked Jack, untieing the rope from his waist.

"After they drugged you," explained Kate, "the man ripped the medallion from my neck and read the back. The inscription told him to come here to the fifth tower. They kept us in a house until the morning and then brought us here, in case they needed my mum's help. When we got here, they realized that the well was too narrow for an adult, so they sent me down on a rope to the bottom."

Kate took a deep breath and carried on. "They told me to put whatever I found at the bottom of the well into a basket I'd been given, and tie it to the end of the rope. Then I was supposed to yank on it to tell them that the treasure was ready. They were supposed to send the rope back down for me. But they didn't. And now they've got the treasure and my mum!"

"Did they say anything about where they were headed?" asked Jack.

"Not exactly," answered Kate, "but I think the man with the gold teeth was going back where he came from."

From something Kate's mum had shouted at the man earlier, Jack knew that he didn't live in Cambodia. There was only one place he could be headed.

"The airport!" said Jack. "We need to try to stop them."

Jack and Kate dashed out of the fifth tower and carefully descended the steep steps. They raced through the courtyard and the two doorways before reaching the grand causeway. At the end of the causeway there was a motorized scooter parked on the dirt road. Jack knew that if he borrowed it the GPF would return it to its rightful owner.

"Quick, hop on!" said Jack as he jumped onto the front of the scooter. Kate clambered on the back and put her arms around Jack's waist. Jack pulled the Magic Key Maker out of his Book Bag and inserted the long rubber tube into the ignition. Instantly, the rubber melted and then hardened again to form a perfect key for the ignition lock. Jack turned the key and the scooter fired up.

"Hold on tight!" he shouted to Kate as the scooter lurched forward and sped off down the road, leaving the Temple of Angkor Wat in its dust.

Chapter 12:
The Airport

"This way!" shouted Kate, above the noise of the scooter's engine. She was pointing towards a large building next to a wide dirt track. "That's the airport!" she yelled.

They turned right into the airport's parking lot and jumped off the scooter. They burst into the building and looked around. Hundreds of passengers, both local and foreign, were either waiting for their flights, or lining up to go through customs and immigration.

Jack and Kate frantically searched the

room. If Kate's mum weren't there, then they'd probably lost her forever.

"Mum!" Kate shouted. She was looking towards the back of the building.

Jack followed her gaze. There, walking towards the back door, was Kate's mother. In front of her was the man with the gold teeth. Behind her was the Thai man, who seemed to be jabbing something into her back.

"Mum!" Kate shouted again. But the noise of the crowded airport drowned her out and Kate's mum didn't turn around.

"What are we going to do?" screamed Kate. "They're going to take my mum away and I can't reach her! We can't get to the other side of the airport without a ticket!"

Jack thought for a moment. "Wait here," he said as he left Kate and moved quietly through the crowds to a place at the front of the immigration line.

He rifled through his Book Bag and pulled out his Voice-Recognition Passport and Trick Ticket. The Voice-Recognition Passport was one of the most useful things the GPF had ever invented. Whenever a secret agent said a name out loud, it transformed the name on the passport to the one the secret agent said. The Trick Ticket, which looked like a boarding card, worked in exactly the same way.

He glanced at the departures sign above and noticed a flight leaving in ten minutes to Thailand. It was flight 101. Jack lifted the Trick Ticket to his mouth and whispered, "Flight 101. Thailand." He then lifted the Voice-Recognition Passport to his lips and said, "Somchai." Jack knew Somchai was a Thai man's name.

"Next," grunted the government official ahead. Jack stepped forward and presented his documentation.

FLIGHT NO.	DESTINATION
101	THAILAND
104	DELAYED

"Thank you," said the official. "Mr. Somchai, is it?" he asked as he looked down at Jack's paperwork. He hesitated and Jack could tell the official was wondering how such a western-looking boy could have a common Thai name. But he couldn't very well ask. Instead, the official compared the name in the passport to the boarding card and paused.

"I hope you've had a nice stay in our country, Mr. Somchai," he said, handing Jack the passport and boarding card and nodding for him to proceed.

"Sure have," said Jack, grabbing back his passport. Jack could see Kate's mum walking outside and onto the runway with the two men.

He dashed through the crowd and placed his Book Bag on the X-ray belt. He hustled through the arches of the security check and picked up his Book Bag, which was waiting for him on the other side. Thanks to the Anti-X-Ray feature on his Book Bag, the security guard checking his bag didn't see his gadgets. All they saw was a fake image of a pack of chewing gum, a couple of books, and a handheld gaming device.

He raced out of the door. There, walking up the steps to a private plane, was Kate's mum, sandwiched between the Thai man, who had a gun in her back, and the man with the gold teeth, who was carrying a black box.

Now what was Jack going to do? This was the kind of situation the GPF always told its agents to try to avoid. It was almost certainly a no-win situation: a hostage situation involving a man with a gun and another with a priceless treasure. How was Jack going to rescue them both and get the bad guys?

Chapter 13:
The Switch

Jack crouched down and ran towards the steps that led to the plane. He reached into his pocket and pulled out a round disc wrapped in black material. Holding this in his hand, he stopped a few feet from the steps of the plane.

"Hey, you!" he yelled up to the man with the gold teeth. The Thai man plunged the gun deeper into Kate's mum's back. Jack could hear her squeal of pain.

The man with the gold teeth slowly turned to look down at Jack from his position at the top of the steps. His eyes

widened in anger and surprise when he
saw Jack standing there.

"Yeah, you!" shouted Jack. "Didn't you
forget something?" He was holding the
covered disc in his hand and waving it in
the air.

"What do you mean?" asked the man,
frowning at Jack.

"Seems like you forgot an important
piece of the treasure!" said Jack, smiling
as if he held an important secret.

"What is it?" he called over to Jack.

"Wouldn't you like to know?" said Jack, taunting the man. "Kate gave it to me," he added, "when I rescued her from the fifth tower."

The man looked at the airport building and spied Kate, who was staring out the window at the runway.

"That's impossible!" he said. "I have it all!"

"Not so," said Jack. "Kate kept a piece back for herself. It's the most important piece, in fact. You can't do anything without it. It's the key to the treasure's power!"

The man furrowed his eyebrows and growled at Jack in anger.

"Of course," said Jack, "you can have it. But only after you release Kate's mum."

He watched the man carefully. He could tell that he didn't know whether to trust Jack or not. But fortunately the man was greedy, which is what Jack was counting on.

"All right, kid!" said the man, his gold teeth shining in the sun. "You can have her, but only after I've looked at it. If it's a hoax," he added, "I'll kill both of you, instantly."

"No way," said Jack, feeling more and more confident. "You're not going to get it until I get Kate's mum."

The man paused for a second. "Chai!" he yelled. With one push, the Thai man threw Kate's mum down the steps and she fell onto the runway. She lay on the ground for a few seconds before slowly picking herself up and looking at Jack.

"Thanks," she mouthed to him as she rushed past him and into the airport building to find Kate.

"Now hand it over!" The man scowled. His patience was wearing thin.

The Thai man turned his attention to Jack. He lifted his gun and pointed it directly at him. Just then, the noise of the engines fired up. Jack didn't have much time. The plane was getting ready to leave.

"Hand it over!" the man yelled again.

Jack could tell he was getting angrier. But Jack still had one more thing to do: he had to get the treasure before the man took it on the plane and it was lost forever. He looked carefully at the black box. It was tied shut with rope.

"OK," said Jack, "but you'll have to catch it!" He tossed the object high in the air, above the man's head.

"No!" screamed the man, dropping the black box in order to catch it with both hands. The disc slipped through his fingers and fell onto the steps of the plane. Both the man with the gold teeth and the Thai man were too busy fumbling for the object to notice that Jack had come up alongside them.

Jack reached into his Book Bag and grabbed The Hook—an expandable hook that allows you to grab things from a distance. Quietly, Jack slipped it through the railings and caught the rope on the black box. He pulled the box through the railings and snatched it away. The treasure was now in Jack's hands.

The man with the gold teeth hurried down the stairs, picked up the object and lifted it towards the sun. "At last, we have the power!" he proclaimed to his henchman, who was now standing by his side. Neither realized that Jack had already snatched the box containing the treasure.

"I wouldn't say that," said Jack as he reached into his Book Bag and pulled out the Net Tosser. The Net Tosser was a ring that when thrown opens up and casts a net. Jack flung it high over the two men. It burst open and fell on top of them, trapping them inside. The Thai man fired his gun at Jack, but the Net Tosser had a built-in "anti-bullet" feature, which prevents any bullets from escaping to the outside. Instead, the bullet pinged around inside the net, with the men cowering for their lives.

The man with the gold teeth shouted from underneath the net. "You'll never be

able to activate the power of the treasure without this!" He lifted the object up towards Jack and unfolded the black material around it. The man looked at it with utter confusion.

"Green Day?" he said, reading the name on the disc. "What is this, some kind of joke?"

"Not at all," said Jack. "It's a great band, in fact. You'll have lots of time to listen to it when you're in prison."

Jack used his Watch Phone to call the local authorities who, in addition to the security guards at the airport, descended on the men within minutes. They lifted the Net Tosser and took the Thai man's gun. Then both of them were cuffed on the spot.

"I'll get you for this!" the man screamed at Jack. "This isn't the last you've seen of me, young man!"

The Thai man spat at Jack and cursed at him in his native language.

Not wanting to let them know that sometimes the evil threats of bad guys actually bother him, Jack just smiled and waved them away.

Chapter 14:
The Resolution

When the commotion died down, Kate burst through the door of the airport and ran onto the runway.

"Jack!" she cried, running towards him, her arms flailing with excitement. "You did it! You saved my mum and the treasure!" She leaped up and kissed him squarely on the lips.

Stunned, Jack stood there, not knowing what to do. The GPF could prepare you for all sorts of occasions, but not one involving a kiss from a girl. Especially a kiss from a girl you liked.

"Thank you so much for saving our lives," said a voice from behind Kate. Jack looked past her. It was Kate's mum. "And for saving the sacred treasure, too."

"I think you'll be needing this," said Jack, handing the box to her. "Hopefully, it will be safer now."

"Don't worry," said Kate's mother. "I'll see to it that no one finds it again." She paused, and Jack could see that she was studying his face. "Would you like to come back to our house and have some tea?" she asked. "I think you probably have a few questions for me."

Jack knew what she was talking about— his brother, Max. He had been waiting for months to find out something, anything, significant about his brother. And here was the woman who was probably the last person to see him before he disappeared. It was as if Max had sent him here to meet her.

"I'd love that," said Jack, giving a deep, relieved sigh.

"Great!" said Kate as she grabbed Jack's hand. Reluctantly, he kept it there as she led him off the runway and they set out for her home.

Chapter 15:
The Final Clue

When they arrived back at Kate's house, they tidied up the kitchen, and Kate's mother poured them all some tea. She sat across from Jack at the kitchen table and began to tell him what she knew about Max.

"I met your brother six months ago, when I was working in Egypt," she said. "I was running a project, much like this one, that involved watching over something sacred. When I got word that someone was planning to steal it, I contacted the GPF and they sent Max to protect it.

"Max was fantastic," she continued. "He was clever and truly passionate about his job. But one day, the thing that he was guarding disappeared, and so did Max. After that, I was reassigned to Cambodia. I truly don't know what happened to your brother," she said. "I'm sorry," she added.

"Is there anything else you can tell me about the mission?" pleaded Jack.

"The only thing I can say is that Max's mission had something to do with a mummy."

"A mummy?" asked Jack.

"That's all I can tell you," said Kate's mum. "I've already said too much."

"Right," said Jack, pushing back his chair and standing up. "It looks as if I've got a bit of research to do on Egyptian mummies." He smiled at Kate's mum. "Thanks for telling me everything you did."

"I hope you do find Max," she said. "And when you do, please tell him I said hello."

"Will do," said Jack. He looked at his Watch Phone. He knew what he needed to do next. He turned to Kate and her mum. "I'd better go," he said.

"Do you have to?" asked Kate, who was wearing a long face.

"Unfortunately, I do," he said, shrugging his shoulders. Jack was a bit sad to be leaving, too. "But you know where to reach me," he said, "and I know where to find you." He smiled at the knowledge that she still had the Transponder.

Kate smiled back, happy to know that there was a chance she might see Jack again.

Jack turned to Kate's mum. "Can I borrow your bedroom?"

She looked puzzled for a moment, but then she realized that GPF agents had to depart in secrecy. She pointed towards a door. "Of course you can," she said. "It's right over there."

Jack gave a final wave to Kate and her mum and stepped into the bedroom. He closed the door and opened the front pouch of his Secret Agent Book Bag. Inside the pocket was a small gray pellet. He pulled it out and threw it on the floor. The pellet broke open, instantly releasing a gray smoke into the air. The smoke began to drift upwards, across his body

and over his eyes. Through the smoke,
Jack could make out a framed photograph
of Kate and her mum.

As soon as the smoke began to move,
Jack tugged on the straps of his Book Bag
and yelled, "Off to England!"

Within an instant, the smoke churned
and swirled around him, sucking him into
its core and transporting him back home.

When he arrived, Jack took a deep
breath. He put his Book Bag under his
bed and climbed into his pajamas. As he

stared up at his Magic Map, thoughts of Egypt and Max swirled around in his head.

He yawned. The time on the clock read 7:31 PM—it was time to get some sleep. After all, he'd had a busy evening. As he got into bed he could hear Lily's loud voice drifting up the stairs.

"And then, Mrs. MacDonald made everyone stay behind after class, just because of what Simon Ryder said . . ."

Jack smiled to himself as he sank into his second deep sleep of the day.

The Pursuit of the
Ivory Poachers:
KENYA

BOOK (6)

The Pursuit of the Ivory Poachers: KENYA

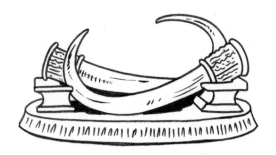

Elizabeth Singer Hunt

Illustrated by Brian Williamson

WEINSTEIN BOOKS

ISBN: 978-1-60286-021-6

First Edition
10   9   8   7   6   5   4

*For my parents, who, like me,
love the African plains*

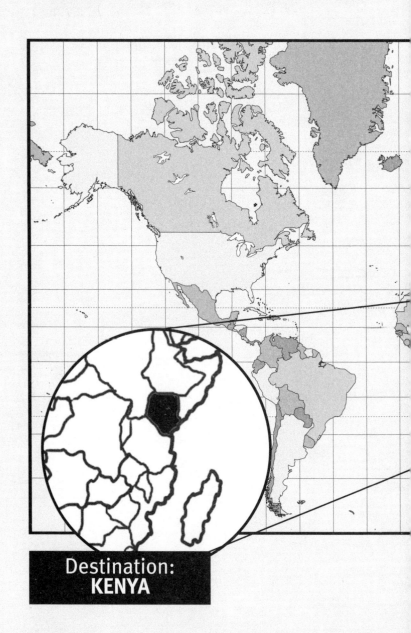

Destination:
KENYA

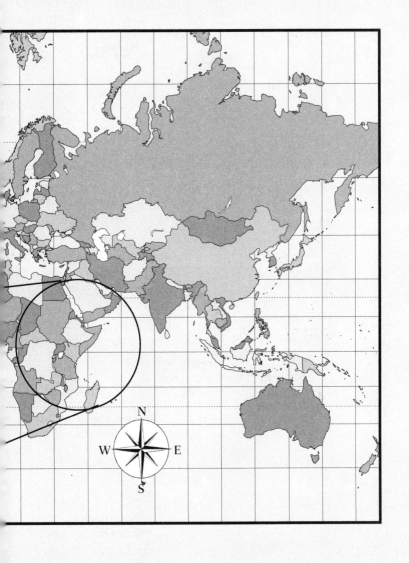

My name is Jack Stalwart. My older brother,

Max, was a secret agent for you, until he

disappeared on one of your missions. Now I

want to be a secret agent, too. If you choose

me, I will be an excellent secret agent and get

rid of evil villains, just like my brother did.

Sincerely,

Jack Stalwart

HIGHLY CONFIDENTIAL

Jack Stalwart was sworn in as a Global Protection Force secret agent four months ago. Since that time, he has completed all of his missions successfully and has stopped no less than twelve evil villains. Because of this he has been assigned the code name "COURAGE."

Jack has yet to uncover the whereabouts of his brother, Max, who is still working for this organization at a secret location. Do not give Secret Agent Jack Stalwart this information. He is never to know about his brother.

Gerald Barter

Gerald Barter
Director, Global Protection Force

THINGS YOU'LL FIND IN EVERY BOOK

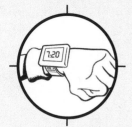

Watch Phone: The only gadget Jack wears all the time, even when he's not on official business. His Watch Phone is the central gadget that makes most others work. There are lots of important features, most importantly the C button, which reveals the code of the day – necessary to unlock Jack's Secret Agent Book Bag. There are buttons on both sides, one of which ejects his life-saving Melting Ink Pen. Beyond these functions, it also works as a phone and, of course, gives Jack the time of day.

Global Protection Force (GPF): The GPF is the organization Jack works for. It's a worldwide force of young secret agents whose aim is to protect the world's people, places, and possessions. No one knows exactly where its main offices are located (all correspondence and gadgets for repair are sent to a special PO Box, and training is held at various locations around the world), but Jack thinks it's somewhere cold, like the Arctic Circle.

Whizzy: Jack's magical miniature globe. Almost every night at precisely 7:30 PM, the GPF uses Whizzy to send Jack the identity of the country that he must travel to. Whizzy can't talk, but he can cough up messages. Jack's parents don't know Whizzy is anything more than a normal globe.

The Magic Map: The magical map hanging on Jack's bedroom wall. Unlike most maps, the GPF's map is made of a mysterious wood. Once Jack inserts the country piece from Whizzy, the map swallows Jack whole and sends him away on his missions. When he returns, he arrives precisely one minute after he left.

Secret Agent Book Bag: The Book Bag that Jack wears on every adventure. Licensed only to GPF secret agents, it contains top-secret gadgets necessary to foil bad guys and escape certain death. To activate the bag before each mission, Jack must punch in a secret code given to him by his Watch Phone. Once he's away, all he has to do is place his finger on the zipper, which identifies him as the owner of the bag, and it immediately opens.

THE STALWART FAMILY

Jack's dad, John

He moved the family to England when Jack was two, in order to take a job with an aerospace company. As far as Jack knows, his dad designs and manufactures airplane parts. Jack's dad thinks he is an ordinary boy and that his other son, Max, attends a school in Switzerland. Jack's dad is American and his mum is British, which makes Jack a bit of both.

Jack's mum, Corinne

One of the greatest mums as far as Jack is concerned. When she and her husband received a letter from a posh school in Switzerland inviting Max to attend, they were overjoyed. Since Max left six months ago, they have received numerous notes in Max's handwriting telling them he's OK. Little do they know it's all a lie and that it's the GPF sending those letters.

Jack's older brother, Max

Two years ago, at the age of nine, Max joined the GPF. Max used to tell Jack about his adventures and show him how to work his secret-agent gadgets. When the family received a letter inviting Max to attend a school in Europe, Jack figured it was to do with the GPF. Max told him he was right, but that he couldn't tell Jack anything about why he was going away.

Nine-year-old Jack Stalwart

Four months ago, Jack received an anonymous note saying: "Your brother is in danger. Only you can save him." As soon as he could, Jack applied to be a secret agent, too. Since that time, he's battled some of the world's most dangerous villains, and hopes some day in his travels to find and rescue his brother, Max.

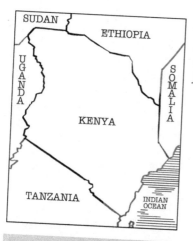

DESTINATION:
Kenya

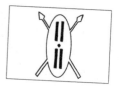

The sun rises at 7:00 AM and sets at 7:00 PM every day in Kenya, because it's located on the equator.

●

The Rift Valley, also called the "Cradle of Mankind," runs through Kenya. It's where many scientists believe 'early man' first evolved and lived.

●

Although Swahili is the national language, many people speak English.

Kenya is on the continent of Africa, the second-largest continent in the world.

●

Nairobi is its capital city.

●

Kenya is a country with beaches, snow-capped mountains, and world-famous safari parks.

The Great Travel Guide

ELEPHANTS: FACTS AND FIGURES

The word elephant means "great arch."

Elephants are the largest land mammals in the world. They can grow to be 13 feet tall and weigh 6 tons.

There are two kinds of elephants: African and Asian.

Elephants have twenty-six teeth, including their tusks. Tusks are made of ivory and have been sought after by hunters for thousands of years.

Elephants can live to be seventy years old. The main threat to their survival is poaching by man. During the 1970s and 1980s, more than eighty per cent of Kenya's elephant population was killed for its ivory.

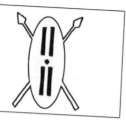

CULTURAL FILE:
The Maasai

The Maasai are a tribe of semi-nomadic people living in eastern Africa.

•

There are roughly 350,000 Maasai living in Kenya.

•

They survive by herding and trading cows, goats, and sheep with other families.

The Maasai live on homesteads. Their homes are made of mud, sticks, grass, cow poo, and urine.

SECRET AGENT GADGET INSTRUCTION MANUAL

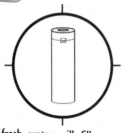

Hydro Pills: The GPF's Hydro Pills are an essential gadget for any secret agent working in extreme heat. Just shake two pills onto the tip of your tongue. Instantly, a burst of fresh water will fill your mouth. Swallow it and feel refreshed.

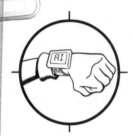

Anti-Intruder Alarm: Built into every secret agent's Watch Phone, the Anti-Intruder Alarm scans the surrounding area to detect when an intruder is nearby. Perfect when you need to get some rest and close your eyes for a while. You'll know there is someone around when your Watch Phone begins to vibrate. The Anti-Intruder Alarm can search up to fifteen feet away. To set the alarm, select the "AI" mode on your Watch Phone.

Transformation Dust:

When you need to change your appearance, even for a short while, use the GPF's Transformation Dust.

Open the green packet and sprinkle some dust onto your head. At the same time, say what you want to become out loud. Within seconds, you will be transformed. To use on other people, just blow the dust over them for the same effect. Consult the back of this handbook for a complete list of transformation options.

Power Pogo:

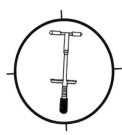

When you need to jump farther than your feet will take you, use the GPF's Power Pogo. The Power Pogo looks like an ordinary pogo stick, but it can catapult you up to fifteen feet into the air. Perfect when you need to get out of harm's way. Just step on and jump.

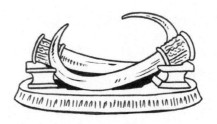

Chapter 1:
The Letter

It was a warm summer evening and Jack
and his mum were sitting at the kitchen
table together. Jack's dad, John, was busy
at work and wouldn't be home until later
that night. As Jack took a bite of his
cottage pie, his mum announced a bit
of news.

"Did I tell you that we got a letter from Max?" she asked Jack.

"Really?" said Jack, only mildly interested. He figured it was another GPF letter designed to make his parents think Max was at a school in Switzerland instead of on assignment.

"It's over here," she said, jumping up from the table and going into the living room. As she rifled through the mail, she went on to explain: "And what's strange is that it's not from Switzerland. It's all the way from Egypt."

"Egypt?" said Jack, nearly choking on a piece of carrot. Why would the GPF fake a letter from Egypt? he wondered. They usually sent Max's letters from an address in Switzerland.

As he was thinking about it, Jack's mum began to read the letter aloud.

Dear Mum, Dad and JAck

You won't Believe iT, but I'M on a field trip iN Egypt. We're learNing about the History of This greAt coUntry and Seeing all Of the anciEnt monumEnts.

Please Tell JacK I miss Him.

Lots of love,

Max

"Isn't that sweet?" said Jack's mum. She was obviously proud of Max for making an effort to learn about the culture of a foreign country. "And look at how busy he is," she added, pointing to the letter. "He must have typed this really quickly."

Jack walked over to his mum and peered at the note where she was pointing. There was a curious mix of uppercase and lowercase letters.

"Can I borrow the letter, Mum?" he asked, trying to hide his excitement.

"Of course, sweetheart," she said. "But take care of it. I'm saving all of Max's letters for his special 'Switzerland scrapbook.'"

Before his mum could start talking again, Jack took the note and ran towards the stairs.

"Thanks!" he shouted as he climbed them two at a time. He reached his bedroom door and dashed inside to his bed. Climbing on top of his duvet, Jack stared carefully at the note.

It looked like a genuine letter. The way it was worded made it sound like Max. And the scribble at the end looked like Max's signature. But two things struck Jack as odd. Except for the handwritten scribble, it was created by a typewriter instead of a computer, and there was something going on with the size of some of the letters.

Jack reached under his bed and pulled out his Secret Agent Book Bag. Using his Watch Phone, he made contact with the GPF. Whenever a secret agent needed to use his or her gadgets when not on a mission, they could ask the GPF for special permission. Sure enough, the GPF quickly sent back the code SUPER CAR.

Jack laughed at how funny that was. He and his brother, Max, loved super cars like Ferraris and Lamborghinis.

Once Jack entered the code, the lock popped open. He reached inside and grabbed his Signature ID. The Signature ID was a three-dimensional rectangular box with a silver viewing screen inside. It was the only gadget in the world that could analyze someone's handwriting and identify its creator from a worldwide file. Whenever a secret agent needed to figure out whether an important document – like a ransom note or an ownership paper – was forged, they used the Signature ID.

For Max's other letters, Louise Persnall was the name given by the Signature ID. Jack knew that Louise was the GPF Director, Gerald Barter's, personal secretary. Hoping this time the letter was for real, Jack crossed his fingers and placed the glass square over the note.

Patiently, Jack waited for the Signature ID to do its work. When it was finished, he heard it beep. He took a breath and looked down at the screen. When he read what was there, his heart skipped a beat.

CREATOR: MAXWELL JOHN STALWART

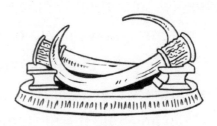

Chapter 2:
The Code

Jack's insides were really tumbling now.
He quickly put the Signature ID back in his
Book Bag. Aside from an anonymous note
telling Jack that Max was in trouble, he'd
received no other communication about
his brother in the past six months.

Jack took another look at the note and
studied the uppercase letters that
shouldn't have been there. He grabbed a
pen and paper from his bedside table and
wrote them down. There weren't many

capital letters, so maybe they formed some sort of a code.

ABTMNNHTAUSOEETKH

Hmm, Jack thought as he stared at the jumble of letters. There was nothing obvious about anything to do with his brother.

When Jack was on a mission in Cambodia, he had received a clue about Max. His brother was supposedly working near a mummy in Egypt. After that tip, Jack did loads of research on mummies, but he still didn't have enough information to pinpoint his exact location.

Now, thought Jack as he stared at the code, he had been given a second chance. He was pretty sure that deep within the code was where Max was and why he was there. If Jack could solve it, he could probably help his brother. If he couldn't, well, Jack didn't even want to think about that.

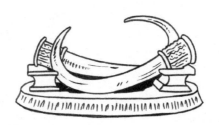

Chapter 3:
The Assignment

Just then, Whizzy started to spin. Startled, Jack looked at the clock next to his little globe. It was already 7:30 PM.

Before Jack could think any more about Max, Whizzy coughed – Ahem! – and spat a jigsaw piece out of his mouth. Leaving his notes behind, Jack raced over to the spot where it landed. He looked at it carefully as he picked it up.

"Now where does this one fit?" he asked, carrying the piece to his Magic

Map. The wooden map of the world that
hung on Jack's wall magically transported
him away on his missions when he placed
the correct country inside.

He lifted the piece up to the left of the
map and tried to match it to Alaska.
When that didn't work, he moved it to
Canada. Going south through North

America and towards Mexico, he waited
for the piece to slip in, but it didn't fit.
He carried on, sliding the piece over South
America, but still no match.

Getting excited that perhaps the country he was going to was actually Egypt, he picked up the piece and placed it over that country on the map. When it didn't match, he slid it over Central Africa and towards Africa's eastern edge. When he reached the coast, the piece fell in. The name "KENYA' appeared and then disappeared into the map.

"Kenya?" said Jack. He knew that Kenya was a place for safari holidays. Maybe a tourist is in trouble, he thought, as he grabbed his Book Bag. He dialed into his Watch Phone for the code of the day. As soon as he received the word – S-A-F-A-R-I – he punched it into the bag's lock and it popped open. Looking through the contents, he made a mental note of his Hydro Pills, Flyboard, and the Lava Laser.

Jack stuffed Max's note into his Book Bag and zipped it shut. He raced back to the

Magic Map, where the light inside Kenya was starting to grow. Knowing that he needed to be focused, Jack thought about Max one more time before sending thoughts of him out of his head.

When the yellow light coming from the African country had filled his room, Jack yelled, "Off to Kenya!" Then the light burst, swallowing him into the Magic Map.

Chapter 4:
The Savannah

When Jack arrived, he found himself alone in an open field. The tall grass under his feet was brown and dry. There was a khaki-colored dirt road to his far right, and the lone tree ahead was just that, all by itself.

From the looks of it, Jack figured he was in the savannah, one of the many types of landscape in Africa. Besides savannahs, Africa also had deserts and tropical rainforests, each with its own kind of exciting wildlife.

Jack opened his Book Bag and pulled out his Google Goggles. The GPF's Google Goggles looked like ordinary swim goggles but they enabled the wearer to see great distances both under the water and on land. He switched them to 'maximum' length, held them up to his eyes, and waited for them to focus.

Far in the distance he could see the animals of the plain. There was a herd of wildebeest making their way across a distant road. Beyond them was a family of giraffe. They were using their long tongues to eat leaves off of some prickly branches. An ostrich leaped into view and dashed across the savannah.

Scanning with the Google Goggles a further thirty degrees, Jack noticed a group of gazelle, a small deerlike animal. They were busy eating something off of the ground, while a group of patient lions watched their every move.

Jack looked at his Watch Phone. It had already adjusted itself to Kenyan time. Thankfully, it was after midday. Knowing that lions typically hunted in the cooler hours of the morning and night, Jack wiped the sweat from his brow. The last thing he needed was an encounter with a pack of hungry wild animals.

Chapter 5:
The Bungling Brit

WHOOSH!

All of a sudden, there was a noise from above.

WHOOSH!

There it was again.

Jack dropped to his knees and aimed his Google Goggles at the sky. Sailing towards him was a red, yellow, and blue-striped hot-air balloon. Hanging underneath the balloon was an enormous wicker basket, and in the basket was a man wearing a floppy hat.

"Hello!" The man waved to Jack from his perch inside the balloon. Jack thought he sounded English.

"Hello!" he shouted again. His arms were flapping wildly as he tried to get control of the flying balloon. "I'm not very good with this thing!" he yelled as the balloon jolted up and down in the sky.

"I say," the man said. "Is your name Jack?"

Jack took a quick look around. Since there wasn't anyone for miles, he figured it was all right to say his name out loud.

"Yes!" he shouted back.

"Jolly good!" the man replied. "I'd hate to have flown all this way to find out your name was Frank!" At this silly joke, the man started roaring with laughter.

Jack watched the man try to steer the balloon to just above where he was standing. With a pull of a cord, he slowly lowered the craft. But instead of landing gently, the balloon's basket hit the ground and tipped over sideways.

"Ahhh!" the man screamed, tumbling out onto the dry grass.

"Are you OK?" asked Jack as he moved quickly to help the man. He was trying not to laugh, but the whole thing was *very* funny.

"Absolutely!" said the man, jumping to a standing position. He straightened his hat, quickly brushing the dirt from his trousers. "Just a bit more practice and I'll have this balloon-thing cracked!" he said.

"Where are my manners?" he exclaimed. "Trevor Dimbleby." He thrust out his hand. "Nice to meet you."

"Nice to meet you too, Trevor," said Jack, shaking the pilot's hand. "What seems to be the problem?" he asked, anxious to hear the reason for his mission.

"Chief Abasi is the one who sent for you," said Trevor. "He's the one with the problem."

"Chief Abasi?" asked Jack, curious to know who he was.

"Chief Abasi," Trevor explained, "is the chief of the local Maasai. He controls the bit of the Maasai Mara where my boss and I run a safari lodge."

Jack knew that the Maasai Mara was one of the biggest safari parks in Kenya and that the Maasai were a group of tribal people who lived off the land.

"Why don't we get a move on?" said Trevor, glancing at his watch. "It's two o'clock and I told the chief that I'd have you back in half an hour."

"Sure thing," said Jack. "But how are we getting there?"

Trevor paused and smiled. Jack looked at the balloon.

"You're joking," said Jack, not entirely confident with Trevor's piloting skills.

"Don't be a scaredy-cat," said Trevor as he started walking towards the craft. "I'm pretty much of an expert in that thing!"

Knowing that he had a few gadgets to help him out, Jack joined Trevor. Trevor was adjusting the temperature of the air, so the balloon could lift off the ground.

"Climb in!" he said to Jack.

Jack grabbed the edge of the basket and pulled himself over the side. He found a space next to the propane gas tanks and watched as Trevor yanked on a lever. A huge plume of flaming hot air shot up above Jack's head and they started to take off. Trevor tugged on the control again and the balloon began to rise even higher.

As they climbed into the sky, they caught a current of wind. The balloon flew upwards and to the east, taking Jack and Trevor to Chief Abasi and the mission ahead.

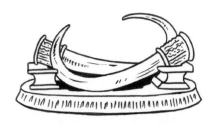

Chapter 6:
The Homestead

After about twenty minutes, Trevor nudged him and pointed to something on the ground. "See that homestead over there?" he said. "That's where we're heading."

Jack lifted his Google Goggles once again, and surveyed the area around the village. There were five small homes made out of mud, a few small buildings, and three fenced-off pens for keeping cattle. Children were playing games, while the women were tending to chores. The entire homestead was surrounded by a thorny fence. It looked quiet and calm; not the kind of place that needed the services of an international secret agent.

When they were close enough, Trevor pulled a string to open the parachute valve. The parachute valve was on top of the balloon. It worked to let the hot air out, so the balloon would drop slowly to the ground. This time when the basket hit the earth, it did so gently. As it tipped over, Jack rolled himself out and Trevor followed him.

"So, where to now?" asked Jack, standing up.

"Over there," said Trevor, pointing to the gate. "Why don't you go ahead? I need to stay here and pack up the balloon."

As Jack walked through the gate and into the enclosure, he saw an African man coming out of one of the huts. He was wearing a red Maasai cloth around his shoulders, and some ornamental beads hung from his head and neck. With the use of a wooden walking stick, he slowly made his way over to Jack. Figuring this was Chief Abasi, Jack extended his hand to greet him.

"*Jambo*," said Jack. Jack knew that '*jambo*' meant hello in Swahili. "*Jina langu ni* Jack Stalwart."

The chief broke into an enormous smile. He was obviously pleased at Jack's attempt to speak the Kenyan language.

Although the Maasai had a language of their own, the man understood enough of what Jack said to respond.

"Welcome," he said, "to my homestead and to my country. I am honored that you have come." Jack was impressed by Chief Abasi's English. He was obviously a well-educated man.

Before Jack could ask, the man got to the point. "The reason I have called for you is that I have discovered a great problem on the Mara."

"What's wrong?" Jack asked. He was wondering what could be so bad in such a peaceful place.

"Why don't we take a walk?" he said, motioning for Jack to follow him out of the homestead. "Walking helps to clear my head," he added.

Jack paused, slightly confused. "OK," said Jack, guessing that whatever the chief had to show him was on the walk.

"Why don't you lead the way?"

The chief used his walking stick to swing round and made his way over to the gate. When Jack reached the gate, he glanced over at Trevor, who was busy chatting on his cell phone. It sounded like he was speaking in Swahili. Spying Jack, Trevor stopped talking and waved. Jack waved back, too. Then he picked up his pace and followed Chief Abasi, who was already ten paces ahead.

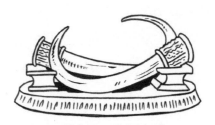

Chapter 7:
The Find

They were only minutes from the camp when Chief Abasi started to talk. "I am a great admirer of the GPF," he said. "I have been following the organization's work." The chief picked up his staff and stuck it into the ground.

Even though he lived in the middle of the African plain, Jack was amazed that Chief Abasi knew about the GPF. "How do you know about us?" asked Jack.

"I have my sources," he replied.

"Despite our simple way of living, I manage to stay on top of world events. Do you have any family?" he asked. Jack was surprised by the sudden change in conversation.

Jack paused for a moment, thinking about home. "I do," he said. "My mum, my dad, and my brother, Max."

"How old is Max?" said the chief.

"He's eleven," said Jack. In fact, his twelfth birthday was coming up. Jack thought about how happy he'd be if he could find Max and bring him home in time for his birthday celebration.

"So, where are we going?" asked Jack, deciding it was best to change the subject away from Max.

"I wanted to take you to the site of the problem, so you could see it with your own eyes," said the chief. He continued to walk ahead through the tall, dry grass. Just to the left, Jack could see eight elephants making their way across the savannah together.

Jack glanced at the temperature on his Watch Phone. It was 90°F. Feeling thirsty, he reached into the front pouch of his Book Bag and plucked out a clear plastic tube. Popping open the top, he shook out two pills and placed them onto the tip of his tongue. Within seconds, they dissolved into a concentrated burst of cool water.

Instantly, Jack felt refreshed. These were the GPF's Hydro Pills – the only way a secret agent could stay hydrated in conditions like this.

"That's where we are headed," said Chief Abasi, lifting his staff and pointing it to a wooden building in the near distance.

Jack thought the building looked like a shed; the kind he had at home in his back garden. As they approached the building, Chief Abasi turned to Jack.

"I must warn you," he said. "What's inside may upset you."

"That's all right," said Jack, trying to sound brave.

The chief turned the handle on the shed door and pulled it wide open. He stood there waiting for Jack to take a look inside. As soon as Jack did, he immediately noticed two things. First, it didn't smell very nice. Secondly, there were lots of flies buzzing around. When his eyes finally adjusted, he knew instantly why Chief Abasi had called the GPF. Leaning against

the walls were the ivory tusks of ten
African elephants.

Sometimes tusks were taken from
elephants that died of natural causes. But
more often elephants were gunned down
and killed so that the poachers could sell
their tusks for money. Some people
believed ivory had healing powers; others
wanted to use it for ornamental carvings.
Jack turned to look at the chief, who was
still outside.

"Now do you understand?" asked Chief Abasi as he shook his head in sadness.

"I do," said Jack. "The people who did this are not warriors," said the chief.

"They are cowards."

"I agree," said Jack, who couldn't believe someone would do something like that. "I promise I'll find out who did this and make sure they never do it again."

"Thank you," said the chief. "Well then" – he stepped away from the shed – "why don't I give you some space? I'm sure that you have some work to do."

Chapter 8:
The Clues

Once Jack had his bearings, he began to look around. The first thing he studied was the tusks themselves. There was nothing unusual about them, except stamped on each with black ink was the name of a faraway country. Jack figured these were the countries buying the tusks, but there was no clue as to who was selling them off.

When he was finished, Jack turned his attention to the outside. Whoever carried the tusks, he reasoned, would have left footprints at the entrance to the shed.

Sure enough, as he stepped outside, Jack spied a collection of footprints. One set of markings was too messy to make out; it was almost as if the person had been shuffling in the dust. The other, however, was so clear that Jack could see a squiggle on the sole of its shoe. A perfect opportunity for the GPF's Footprint Finder to do its stuff.

He grabbed the gadget from his Book Bag and turned it on by pulling on the ends of the yellow stick. Slowly, he moved the wand over the markings, giving it just enough time to register the print. Instantly, the Footprint Finder revealed the shoe's brand and size.

BOOT UNKNOWN, SIZE 11

Weird, Jack thought. The Footprint Finder almost never failed to identify a

shoe. It must be from a shoe that's custom-made.

He followed the footprints as they travelled from the shed to a nearby road. There they stopped at a set of four tire marks. Luckily for Jack, he didn't need a gadget to tell him what made these; he knew almost everything there was to know about cars. Based on the width of the axle and the tire's tread, these marks could only come from one kind of car: a four-wheel drive truck. Unfortunately for Jack, this was one of the most common types of vehicles on the African plain.

When Jack was finished, he joined Chief Abasi. "I'm done," he said.

"Did you find anything interesting?" asked the chief.

"Yeah," said Jack, "it looks like more than one person put the tusks in the shed. After that, they drove off in a four-wheel drive truck."

"Interesting," said the chief, considering what Jack had said. As if he was thinking about what that meant, Chief Abasi said,"I think you should meet Mr K next."

"Mr K?" asked Jack.

"His real name is Jasper Kendall," said the chief. "He runs Mr K's Safari Lodge, the largest safari camp in the Maasai Mara." "He and I have an arrangement of sorts," he added. "I let him run his business on Maasai land. In return, he lets us entertain and sell souvenirs to his guests."

"Do you think he'll know something about the poachers?" asked Jack.

"I am not sure," said the chief. "But what I do know is that Jasper is extremely well-connected; he has his finger into most things going on in and around the Mara."

"Great idea," said Jack, who agreed that a meeting would be wise. "Where exactly is Mr K's?"

"It's a short drive from the village," said the chief. "Trevor can take you and arrange for you to spend the night."

Jack hadn't even thought about the

time. He glanced at his Watch Phone. It was 5:30 PM. Since he knew the sun set at 7:00 PM, he didn't have enough daylight to solve the crime. He was going to have to spend the night at Mr. K's and carry on with his investigation in the morning.

As long as Jack stayed on a mission no longer than forty-eight hours, the GPF could return him to his bedroom at 7:31 PM. Beyond that they'd have to fake a reason for Jack being gone. That's what they did for Max. They engineered it so he was in a "boarding school."

"Shall we meet up again tomorrow?" suggested Jack.

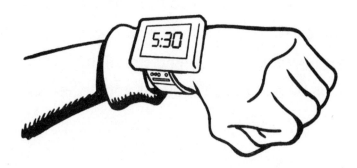

"Yes," said Chief Abasi. "Trevor can pick you up in the morning and bring you back to the homestead."

"Great," said Jack. "That sounds like a plan."

Just then, Trevor pulled up in a jeep. Chief Abasi looked surprised at his arrival.

"Hello there," said Trevor, who was no longer wearing his hat. "I borrowed a car. I figured the two of you could use a lift."

"Stopped using the balloon, I see," said Jack, joking with Trevor. Jack climbed into the back of the car, leaving the front seat for the chief. "Aren't you coming?" he asked Chief Abasi, who was lingering behind.

"No thanks," he said. "I'd prefer to walk. Enjoy your visit with Mr K." He nodded his head to say goodbye and then turned to walk in the opposite direction.

Trevor crunched the gears, then slammed

his foot on the accelerator. As they tore off, Jack thought about Trevor – he hoped he was a better driver than he was a balloon pilot, but held on to his Book Bag, just in case.

Chapter 9:
The Safari Camp

Trevor and Jack had driven over the dusty plain for half an hour when Jack noticed a large campsite in the distance. There was an enormous wooden lodge in the middle surrounded by dozens of oversized green tents. Around the perimeter was an electric fence. Probably, Jack thought, to keep the lions away.

"That's Mr K's," said Trevor, pointing at the camp.

As they pulled up at the entrance, Jack

spied a large sign. It was written in big, bold letters. Inside the middle of the K was a drawing of a lion.

Beside the sign was an armed guard dressed in an olive shirt and trousers. Recognizing Trevor, he nodded and then let them pass. Trevor drove down the long path towards the lodge itself. He parked the jeep in a space marked 'reserved' and turned off the engine. Almost at the same time, a large man came out. Wearing a brown cowboy hat and a checked shirt, the man looked like he belonged more on the plains of Texas than that of Kenya.

"Hi there!" he bellowed. "How are you doing?" He sounded like he was from South Africa. Jack guessed that Trevor had called ahead and that he knew to expect them.

"So glad you could come," he said excitedly. "Welcome to my home. We call it Mr K's," he added, "after the first letter in my last name, Kendall." He looked over to Jack with a cheesy grin. "You get it?" he said.

Jack looked at the man and forced a smile. There was something about Jasper

that wasn't quite right. When he glanced down at his choice in footwear, Jack was shocked. He was wearing boots made with the skin of an endangered sea turtle.

"I thought killing sea turtles for their skins was against the law," said Jack, furrowing his brow in disapproval. He couldn't forget his duties with the GPF.

"These things?" he said, brushing Jack off. "These are so old," he said. "I've had them since before you were born!" Quickly changing the subject, Mr K carried on.

"Why don't you come in and have a look around?" Jasper slapped Jack on the back and led him down a gravel path towards the front door.

"Must be off," said Trevor as he climbed into the jeep. Trevor started the car up and began to back out. Before Jack could say goodbye, he'd sped away.

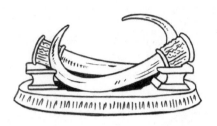

Chapter 10: The Meal

"Now," said Jasper, slapping Jack on the back a second time, "let's go inside!"

Jasper led Jack under the covered walkway and through the front door. When they entered the lobby, the first thing that caught Jack's eye was the elephant tusks. There were two decorated ivory teeth perched on a wooden stand in the corner.

Sensing that Jack was a bit stunned, Jasper explained. "They were given to me by the previous owners. I'd never kill an elephant for its ivory." Jasper coughed.

Uh-huh, thought Jack. He's wearing boots from an endangered species and he's got two tusks proudly displayed in the front hall of his lodge. Definitely, Jack decided, a guy who needs to be watched.

As they moved into the lodge, Jack noticed several young men doing a traditional Maasai jumping dance. Jack knew that Maasai showed their strength as warriors by jumping as high as they could. Remembering what Chief Abasi had said, Jack figured they were there to entertain Jasper's guests.

The two of them moved through the hall and towards a wooden deck outside. Almost as soon as he stepped onto the platform, Jack was overwhelmed by the wildlife. Black and white colobus monkeys were jumping from tree to tree. A spider the size of his dad's hand sat in the middle of its web just above Jack's head.

He walked over to the railing and
looked over the edge. The deck was
perched ten yards above a river below.
There were some hippos sitting low in the
water with their ears and eyes peeking
out. A handful of baby crocodiles were
scurrying across a log as their parents
snapped up whatever food they could.

"Why don't you have a seat?" said
Jasper, motioning for Jack to join him

at a round wooden table and chairs
nearby.

Jack did just that, being careful to
watch not only his surroundings but also
his host.

"So," said Mr K, "Chief Abasi told me
about those tusks. Shame about the
elephants." At that comment, Jasper
Kendall lifted his feet and placed them on
the chair next to Jack. Since the shoes

weren't that far away, Jack couldn't help but notice a squiggly line on the soles, just like the one he'd seen at the shed.

Jack's eyes widened. He needed to be careful. There was a chance he was sitting across from one, if not the leader of, the poachers. He cleared his throat.

"Yes," said Jack, trying to keep his cool.

"It's terribly upsetting." He didn't want Jasper to know that he'd seen the boots.

"Do you know who could have done this?" he asked.

"Gosh," said Jasper, almost sincerely. "I can't think of anyone."

"Well, why do you think someone would do it?" asked Jack.

"People round here don't make a lot of money," he explained, "and poaching is one of the best ways to get it."

Hmmm, thought Jack. Jasper wasn't admitting to anything. Jack didn't have enough evidence. He couldn't have him arrested just because of his boots. For all Jack knew, that squiggly line could be on any number of boots in the area. He was going to have to do better. He was going to have to catch Jasper Kendall in the act.

As Jack was thinking, a waiter came over and presented him with a plate of food. "Jambo," he said as he smiled down at Jack and placed the meal on the table.

"I ordered you some dinner," said Jasper, smiling.

Jack looked down at the skewer of alternating vegetables and gray meat.

"What is it?" asked Jack. He'd heard that in Africa people ate all sorts of things like zebra, crocodile, and wildebeest.

"An ostrich kebab," said Mr K.

Jack eyes popped open. The last thing

he wanted to do was eat that. Seeing Jack's reaction, Mr K roared with laughter.

"I'm actually not hungry right now," said Jack, trying to be polite. "Maybe I can take it back to my room?"

"Of course," said Jasper. He motioned to the waiter to wrap Jack's dinner.

"Just one more question," said Jack. "Have you noticed anyone acting strangely around here?"

"No one that I can think of," said Jasper.

"Well," Jack said, thinking he'd gotten all he was going to get out of Jasper, "I think I'd better head off to bed." He picked up his food.

"Let me show you to your room," said Jasper, standing to join Jack.

Jasper led Jack out of the dining room, through the lodge, and back outside.

Passing several large green tents in the compound, they arrived at one near the other end of the river bank.

"This is where you'll be sleeping tonight," said Jasper as he walked with Jack to a small wooden deck outside the tent opening. "I think you'll agree that our tents are pretty luxurious."

Jack pushed back the flaps to the tent. He walked in and couldn't believe his eyes. It was as big as his bedroom at home.

"There's a hot water bottle in your bed already," said Jasper. "It gets pretty cool at night. Electricity runs on a generator," he added. "Lights go off at eight-thirty and don't come on again until five in the morning."

Jack looked down at his Watch Phone. It was 7:30 PM. "Great," he said to Mr K, "that'll give me an hour to do some work."

"Sleep tight," said Jasper as he let himself out. "Don't let the bed bugs bite." He gave Jack a big wink and pulled the flap to Jack's tent closed behind him.

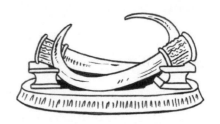

Chapter 11:
The Breakthrough

Figuring he couldn't do any more on the case until tomorrow, Jack climbed onto the bed and got out Max's note. He looked at the uppercase letters again and thought about how to decipher the code. In his training, the GPF had taught him how to unscramble an "anagram." Anagrams were jumbled letters that when put back into the right order spelled a word.

He wrote out the letters again:

ABTMNNHTAUSOEETKH

Figuring the first thing Max would want to tell him was his location, he thought about places in Egypt where mummies could be found. There was the Valley of the Kings, but the letters in that word didn't match Max's code. He then thought about Thebes, where the Valley of the Kings was located. Sure enough, those letters were there. He crossed them out one by one.

ABTMNNHTAUSOEETKH

Then he took the letters that were left and wrote them out again:

AMNNTAUOTKH

65

Now, Jack reckoned, there was a pretty good chance that what remained spelled the name of the mummy close to where Max was working. Jack tried to remember all the tombs found in the Valley of the Kings. There was the tomb of Seti and Siptah. Then there were at least seven tombs belonging to Ramses. But, those names didn't crack the code. And Jack couldn't remember any more. The only way Jack could solve this riddle was to look through his ancient Egypt book, which unfortunately was at home.

Knowing he couldn't do anything else, Jack put his brother's letter back in his Book Bag. Popping one of the GPF's Micro Brushes into his mouth, he swirled it around, letting it brush his teeth. When it was finished, it dissolved in his mouth. Since he didn't have any pajamas, Jack decided to sleep in his normal

clothes. He kept his Book Bag on for safekeeping.

After setting his Anti-Intruder Alarm, Jack crawled under the covers and lay on his side. Once he was comfortable, he closed his eyes and let his mind drift off to sleep. After all, he had some bad guys to catch in the morning.

Chapter 12:
The Intruder

Sometime in the early morning, Jack was woken by a strong vibration on his wrist. Uh-oh, he thought. It was his Watch Phone's Anti-Intruder Alarm. It was telling him that there was somebody in the room.

Jack lay completely still and made sure his breathing was steady and slow.

Because it was dark and he couldn't see, the only senses he had were hearing and smell. He made use of both – as best

he could – and tried to figure out who
was sneaking around inside his tent.

Oddly enough, whoever it was, barely
made a sound. Usually if someone was
there, you could hear them breathe. Or
smell their perfume. But there was no
obvious scent. There was however a gentle
noise. It sounded like it was coming from
above Jack's head.

Sssssssss.

Ssssssss.

It was coming closer.

Sssssssss.

Sssssssss.

Thinking he had an idea of what it was, Jack slowly rose to a kneeling position, turning on his Everglo Light. Even though it looked like a small part of his Watch Phone, the Everglo Light could send a bright beam for at least fifteen feet.

At first he couldn't see anything because the intruder was the same green color as the tent, and Jack's eyes were getting used to the bright light. But when they did, he nearly jumped from the shock.

It was an African boomslang, one of the deadliest snakes in the world, and it was lowering itself down from a light in the ceiling, towards Jack on the bed below.

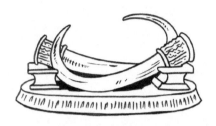

Chapter 13:
The Idea

Before Jack could do anything, the snake
had coiled itself to within three feet of his
face. As Jack looked up, he stared into the
snake's eyes. They were black and cold.
Boomslangs were hemotoxic, which
meant they could inject a poison that
could make you bleed to death. And they
were aggressive – one move from Jack
and the snake would strike.

Since boomslangs were tree-dwelling
snakes, the only way Jack could save

himself was to pretend he was a tree. He slowed his breathing down and sat totally still.

Closing his eyes, Jack waited. The first thing he felt was the snake's cold body brushing against his nose. Then he felt it slide across his face. Slithering over his right shoulder, the snake made its way around his Book Bag and down the length of his back. Although it was travelling fairly quickly for a boomslang, it wasn't quick enough as far as Jack was concerned. It took all of his energy and concentration

not to move. But he had to remain still, or the snake would bite.

Finally, Jack felt the snake slide off of him and onto his mattress. As soon as he heard its heavy body thump onto the floor, he opened his eyes and looked around. The flap to his tent was wide open. The snake being in his room was no accident – somebody put it in there.

He looked over his shoulder and spied the snake's tail going under his bed. Thinking this was a perfect opportunity to escape, Jack carefully stood up and, using the beam from the Everglo Light, leaped as far as he could away from the bed. He hurried to the opening of the tent and stopped to look back. The boomslang was coming out from under the bed. Not wanting to come face-to-face with the creature again, Jack quickly headed out through the tent flap.

Now that he was outside, Jack decided the safest place for him was the lodge. Although the tents were dark, the main lodge was lit throughout the night. With the beam of his Everglo Light guiding him, he made his move. Just to his left, he could hear hippos burrowing themselves into the bank. From somewhere above came the strange sound of an unknown animal. Jack reckoned he'd seen enough of the local wildlife for one night, and hurried towards the main building as quickly as he could.

Chapter 14:
The Transfer

"Jack!" said a voice from up ahead. Thanks to the glow of his torch, Jack could see that it was Jasper Kendall heading towards him. "What are you doing here?" he asked, seeming surprised. "It's a bit early to be out and about, isn't it?"

Yeah, right, thought Jack, who was thinking it was more than a coincidence that Jasper was up this early, too. Maybe he was the one who had put the snake in Jack's tent. Not wanting to let him in on his private thoughts, Jack just shrugged. "I wanted to use the lights in the main lodge to do some work."

"I see," said Jasper. He didn't seem convinced by Jack's excuse. "Why don't I take you there?" he said, leading Jack by the arm. "Shall I call Trevor and tell him that you'll be ready . . . a bit earlier than expected?"

"That would be nice," said Jack.

They soon reached the main building and Jasper phoned Trevor. It wasn't long before he arrived. He pulled up in the darkened car park. After all, it was only 6:00 AM.

"Morning," Trevor said. "I was thinking I'd take you on a safari drive. It's too early to see the old man anyway," he said, meaning Chief Abasi. "He's probably still asleep. But the animals, on the other hand, are just starting to wake up."

Jack thought that was a great idea. Any opportunity to learn about the animals, especially the elephants, could only help with the investigation. He also wanted to search for clues that would tie Jasper Kendall to the crime.

"Excellent idea," said Jack as he climbed into the front seat. Jack was impressed by Trevor's new Land Rover. He'd ridden in the same kind of vehicle once with his dad at a local motor show. "Nice car," Jack said.

"Thanks," said Trevor. "I got it in Mombasa."

Jack turned in his seat and looked at Mr K, who was waiting at the edge of the car park. He waved goodbye and gave Jack one of his cheesy grins. *I'll get you*, thought Jack as he waved back. *It's just a matter of time.*

Chapter 15:
The Lion's Den

They'd driven for half an hour in darkness when Trevor piped up. "There's a place nearby where you can see the sunrise and watch the animals," he said.

"Sounds great," said Jack, who was looking forward to a break. After all, he'd had a stressful morning.

After a few minutes, Trevor shifted the car down a gear. "This is the place I told you about," he said as the Land Rover began to climb a steep hill. The car rocked back and forth as it made its way over some jagged rocks. "You'll love the view from up here." He sounded very excited.

When the car heaved over the ridge, Trevor drove onto a flatter piece of land. With the sun beginning to rise, Jack could make out some trees lining the top of the hill. Dotting the ground were what looked like small- to medium-sized rocks. Trevor put the car into neutral.

As Jack looked around, he noticed something odd. There weren't any animals here. What was Trevor thinking? Jack said to himself. Then he heard what sounded like a lion's yawn.

Squinting, Jack could just make out some larger shapes underneath the trees. As the sun's light grew brighter by the second, things became clearer. There were six adult lions lying down on their bellies. Four of them were female; two of them were male. Jack knew this because two had magnificent manes of hair. Jack wouldn't have been so worried if it weren't for the fact that the Land Rover didn't have any doors on its sides.

"Trevor," said Jack, not wanting to sound scared, "isn't this a bit risky? I'd like to see some wild animals," he added, "but maybe not lions that are this close."

Trevor turned to Jack. "Get out," he said. But he didn't say it kindly; he said it with a sinister snarl.

"What?" said Jack, who wasn't sure he'd heard Trevor correctly.

Trevor opened the glove box in front of Jack. He reached in and pulled out a knife in a brown leather sheath. As Trevor slid the cover off with his other hand, he glared at Jack.

"You heard me," he growled. "Get out! And if you don't," he added, "I'll have to use this." Trevor waved the knife in Jack's face so he could see its razor-sharp edge.

Jack was stunned. What was going on? Where was the friendly Trevor he knew? And why was he holding a knife in Jack's face?

"I've been collecting these tusks for weeks," Trevor explained. "And then Chief Abasi had to go and find them on one of his little "walks." Now, I have to find more ivory," he explained. "My Far Eastern buyers are desperate for their goods, and I don't need the likes of you getting in the way."

Jack almost couldn't talk from surprise. "But I thought—" said Jack, thinking about Jasper Kendall and the bootprints he'd found at the shed.

"What, that Jasper Kendall had something to do with it?" he snarled. "That guy couldn't pick his nose if it weren't for me! I knew a little busybody like you would come sniffing around the shed if it was ever found," he explained, "so I put Jasper's boots on and made some nice tracks. Looks like it worked. Otherwise you wouldn't be here with me."

Jack thought back to when he first met Trevor. Trevor made it seem like he was a bit of a clown . . . the floppy hat, his wacky way of piloting the balloon, the way he talked. That was all just a trick to make Jack think he was a nice guy, not a cold-hearted ivory poacher!

"I tried to get rid of you last night," Trevor went on, "but somehow you managed to escape. This time," he added, with a snigger, "I think the lions will do a better job."

Of course, Jack thought. Trevor must have snuck back into the camp and put the snake in his tent. It would have been very easy for him to do. After all, they were used to seeing him around Mr K's.

Jack didn't have much time. He pulled his thoughts together. "But how can you kill innocent animals?" he said, trying to distract Trevor. As he spoke, he took what looked like a coin out of his pocket and let it drop to the floor of the Land Rover.

"There's only one simple answer to that question," said Trevor. "Money . . . Now get out!"

Jack thought about his options. Unfortunately for him there wasn't a gadget that could get him out of a situation involving a knife. There was only one thing to do, and that was to climb out of the car and take his chances with the lions.

Chapter 16:
The Trees

With the sun nearly awake, Jack could see finally what he was up against. The lions were now standing on all fours. They were watching Jack as he got out of the car.

"Trevor," said Jack as he stepped out and onto the dirt. "I'm warning you. Don't do this. African elephants are already endangered. Killing more will just make matters worse."

Trevor laughed one last dramatic laugh – he didn't care at all. He revved the engine and slipped it back into gear, then peeled away from the spot and left Jack without any protection.

"ROOOOAAARR!"

Quickly, Jack turned around to see one of the male lions licking his chops. The females were gathering together. Jack knew that lions hunted in the morning hours, which meant that they were probably looking at Jack as easy food. He didn't have much time to act. He was going to have to get out of there before they attacked.

Taking off his Book Bag, Jack crouched on the ground. The female lions were beginning to surround him, since they did all of the hunting. With animals on all sides, there was only one gadget that could help Jack.

The GPF's Power Pogo was a pogo stick like no other. With one bounce, it could catapult you up to fifteen feet high.

Jack grabbed the life-saving gadget, strapped his Book Bag back on, and placed his hands and one foot on the Power Pogo. He looked at the lions. The female lions were inching closer while the male lions were waiting patiently under the trees.

"ROOOOAAARR!

Like lightning, the lionesses sprang into action, pushing with their strong hind legs to leap forward. They were charging at top speed in an attempt to bring Jack down! Quickly, Jack lifted his other foot and jumped onto the pogo stick for its first bounce. When it hit the ground, it flew up into the air.

BOING!

One of the lion's paws just missed Jack's feet as he rocketed into the sky,

then came crashing back to the ground.
Luckily for Jack, he landed just to the
right of the pride of lions, who were
scrambling to reach him.

BOING!

This time he sprung even further. One
more time, thought Jack, and he'd be next
to the trees.

BOING!

The Power Pogo thrust him towards an
acacia tree. As he came down, he grabbed
onto one of its branches and held on. His
feet were dangling down. The Power Pogo
fell to the dusty ground, almost hitting one
of the male lion's head.

"ROOOOAAAARR!"

The male lion wasn't happy. Using the
strength in his arms, Jack pulled himself
onto a branch inside the tree. Perched
there for safety, he glanced down at the
lions below. Their "easy" breakfast had

completely disappeared. Jack smiled.
Things were finally going his way.

Taking a moment, Jack remembered
what Trevor had said. He needed more
ivory. Guessing that's where Trevor was
off to now, Jack looked at his Watch
Phone and punched a few buttons. The
Transponder that he'd dropped in
Trevor's car was showing a location

just ten miles away. Since the blinking light wasn't moving, Jack started to worry.

Jack had to get to Trevor before he killed another elephant. He looked out the other side of the tree from where he was sitting. There was a gentle drop from the hill to the savannah. Peering through the branches at the lions, he saw that they had given up on catching him. The pride was heading somewhere else in search of food. Lowering himself down, he collected his gadget, packed it away, and scrambled through some bushes to the top of the slope. He slid down it towards the flatter land below. Perfect terrain, Jack thought, for one of his favorite gadgets. It was the GPF's Flyboard and it was waiting for him in his Book Bag.

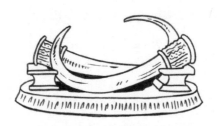

Chapter 17:
The Confrontation

After snapping the Flyboard together, Jack hopped on. Punching the "air" button on his Watch Phone, the jets fired up and Jack and the Flyboard took off. Given the distance and the speed he was travelling, Jack worked out he would arrive at the Land Rover within moments.

He soon saw Trevor's car up ahead, and it looked as if he was just in time. Directly across from the car was a family of elephants. They were bumping into

trees and grasping at branches with their trunks. Trevor was standing up in the vehicle with another man. It looked like the waiter from Mr K's lodge – the one who served Jack his ostrich kebab. So, that's Trevor's accomplice, thought Jack. That's who left the set of messy footprints at the shed.

The two men were wearing hunter's vests and pointing their guns towards one of the female elephants.

"No!" screamed Jack, urging the
Flyboard to go faster.

But Trevor and the other man couldn't
hear him; he was still half a mile away.
They leaned their ears on the guns and
looked through the sights.

"Stop!" yelled Jack.

At that last shout, Trevor must have heard him, because he lifted his head and looked in Jack's direction. By the time both men had registered Jack's arrival, he was nearly there.

"You?" snarled Trevor, clearly unhappy to see that Jack had escaped a second time. "What are you doing here?" he yelled. "Go away! We have some business to do."

"No, you don't," said Jack. "I'm not going to let you kill these elephants!"

"Oh, yeah?" said Trevor, swinging his gun so that it was now pointing at Jack.

Jack flinched.

"Hapana!" the other man yelled in Swahili, aiming his gun at Jack, too. The female elephant sensed the danger and was leading her family in the other direction.

As Trevor put his head down on the gun, ready to fire, Jack pulled his Lava Laser out of his bag. Even though it looked like

an ordinary pencil, the GPF's Lava Laser
was powerful enough to make metal burn
as hot as lava, so that whoever was
touching it would have to drop it.

Trevor put his finger on the trigger. Jack
fired the Lava Laser. A ray of light shot
out of the gadget and struck the metal on
Trevor's gun. Almost instantly, the gun
started to glow orange with heat, burning
Trevor's hands.

"Owwww!" he yelled in agony, dropping the hot metal object.

"*Hapana!*" the Kenyan man yelled, lowering his face to his gun. He was about to fire.

But Jack and the Lava Laser got him, too.

"Ahhhh!" he howled, shaking his hands and trying to cool them. Jack guessed that a cry of pain sounded the same in Swahili as it did in English.

Realizing that they weren't going to kill either Jack or the elephants, the two men dropped in their seats. They were going to start up their car. Trevor tried to turn the key in the ignition, but his hands were too sore and blistered to touch anything.

"Arrgh!" he yelled, obviously disgusted with what was happening.

Panicked and desperate, the two men jumped out. They started to run in different directions. Jack reached into his pocket and pulled out his Transformation Dust. He opened the packet and directed the Flyboard over to the waiter from Mr K's lodge.

"Rhinoceros," Jack said as he blew some of the dust onto the man's face.

"Kifaru?" the waiter said, repeating the word for rhinoceros in Swahili. As the dust flew into his face, he coughed, spat, and shook his head. Almost instantly, he was transformed into one of the most hunted and endangered African animals – the black rhino. Jack then sped over to Trevor, who was sprinting as far as he could, but not fast enough.

"Please, don't!" Trevor screamed as he looked at his accomplice and realized what Jack was about to do. "Noooo!"

"Elephant," said Jack as he blew the dust. On that very spot, Trevor was turned

into a two-ton female elephant. Trevor
lifted his trunk and blew a sound of fury.

"Now," said Jack, pleased with himself.
"Let's see how you like being a hunted
animal."

Although Jack would have loved to keep
them that way forever, he knew the GPF's

Transformation Dust would only last an hour. No problem, thought Jack. It was a clever enough way to catch the poachers and teach them a lesson at the same time.

Jack phoned the Kenyan police, who arrived fairly quickly, but not soon enough for both Trevor and the waiter, who were being sniffed at by a pack of hyenas.

Once the criminals had changed back to themselves, the police officers arrested them and hauled them off.

"You're going to pay for this, kid!" yelled Trevor as the van door shut behind him.

No, thought Jack to himself. *You're the one who's going to pay.*

Chapter 18:
The Find

Now that the bad guys were locked up, it was time to pay a visit to Chief Abasi. After all, Jack was supposed to meet him this morning and he was already late.

He jumped on his Flyboard and headed for the homestead. As he zoomed towards the gate of the Maasai village, Chief Abasi came out of a hut to greet him.

"Hello, Jack," he said, using his stick to walk over. "Has anything happened since we last spoke?"

"You wouldn't believe the morning I've had!" said Jack. "I was nearly bitten by a poisonous boomslang and mauled by a pack of lions!"

Chief Abasi's eyes widened at the news.

"But everything is all right now," said Jack. "I caught Trevor and a waiter from Mr K's trying to kill more elephants. They were the poachers responsible for those tusks in the shed."

Chief Abasi wobbled on his feet before taking a step back. He was obviously in a bit of shock. "I can't believe this," said the chief. "Trevor was a trusted friend of the Maasai people."

"Unfortunately, I don't think Trevor was anybody's friend," said Jack. "He pretended to be nice so nobody would suspect him of the crime. But Trevor's locked up now, so he'll have plenty of time to think about what he's done."

Chief Abasi shook his head. "Well then," he said to Jack, "we owe you and the GPF a great deal of thanks. You've rid our area of some nasty poachers and the elephants here in Kenya will be safer thanks to your efforts."

"No problem," said Jack, who was pleased with himself. "I'm just happy I could help." He held out his hand. "If there are any more problems, give me a call."

"I will," said the chief, putting his hand in Jack's. "Be safe in your travels. And to help guide you, I would like to give you a gift." Chief Abasi left Jack for a moment and walked to his hut.

When he returned, he had a beaded necklace in his hands. "This is for good luck," he said, handing it to Jack. "And for the luck of your family."

Little did the chief know, thought Jack, how much luck the Stalwart family actually needed. As Jack looked down at the red necklace, he thought about his brother Max.

Jack took the object and smiled. "Thank you," he said as he placed it around his neck. "I'll treasure it always." Jack waved goodbye to the chief and stepped on his Flyboard.

Leaving the homestead behind, he flew across the hot plains and stopped near a cluster of bushes. He packed his gadget away, and after pushing a few buttons on his Watch Phone, closed his eyes and yelled, "Off to England!" Within moments Jack was transported home to his bedroom.

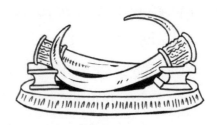

Chapter 19:
The Breakthrough

As soon as he arrived, Jack grabbed the
book on ancient Egypt off of his bookcase
and sat down with it and his brother's
note. He flicked through the pages and
found one with a list of all the tombs in
Thebes, then laid out what was left of the
code again:

AMNNTAUOTKH

Then Jack compared the tomb names with the letters in the code. The first name on the list was Merenptah, but that didn't work. Scrolling down, he tried to match every name with the anagram, but nothing seemed to fit. By the time he got to the last name, he didn't hold out much hope. Jack wrote out the letters anyway. After all, King Tut was the most famous mummy in the world.

TUTANKHAMON

As he was writing, he realized that nearly every letter fit with the anagram from Max's note. The only problem was that in the book Tutankhamun was spelled with a "u' instead of the "o' that was in Max's code. Drat, thought Jack. Maybe he was wrong. Maybe the letters spelled another mummy's name.

But it was so close. Perhaps, wondered Jack, there was another spelling. He knew this was common when it came to ancient names for people and places. Feeling excited, he raced to his computer and punched the name Tutankhamun into the search field. Three different spellings for the famous boy king showed up.

One of them was spelled with an "o."

Jack looked down at the necklace that Chief Abasi had given him. "Thanks," he whispered to the man who had given him the necklace and his incredible good luck.

TUTANKHAMON

It was a perfect match.

The Puzzle of the
Missing Panda:
CHINA

BOOK (7)

The Puzzle
of the
Missing Panda:
CHINA

Elizabeth Singer Hunt

Illustrated by Brian Williamson

WEINSTEIN BOOKS

For Ann and Robert Hunt

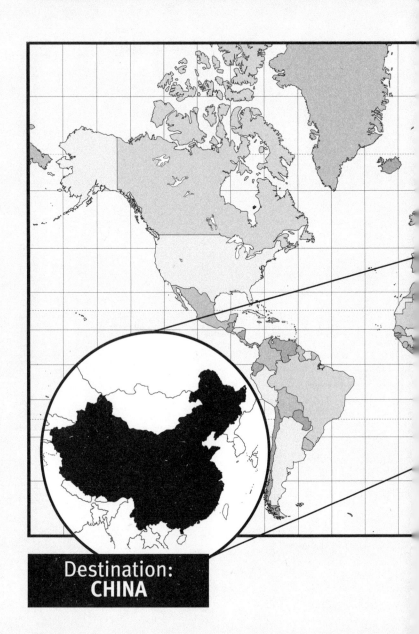

Destination:
CHINA

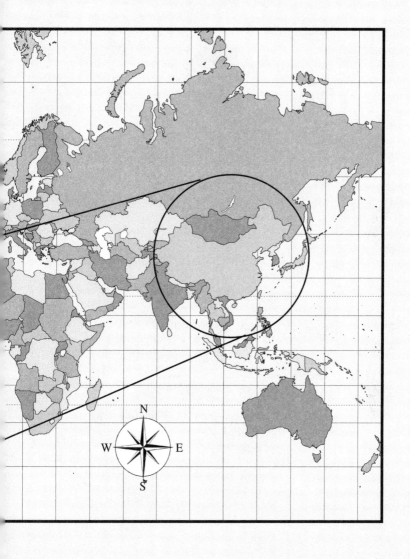

My name is Jack Stalwart. My older brother,

Max, was a secret agent for you, until he

disappeared on one of your missions. Now I

want to be a secret agent too. If you choose

me, I will be an excellent secret agent and get

rid of evil villains, just like my brother did.

Sincerely,

Jack Stalwart

HIGHLY CONFIDENTIAL

Jack Stalwart was sworn in as a Global Protection Force secret agent four months ago. Since that time, he has completed all of his missions successfully and has stopped no less than twelve evil villains. Because of this he has been assigned the code name "COURAGE."

Jack has yet to uncover the whereabouts of his brother, Max, who is still working for this organization at a secret location. Do not give Secret Agent Jack Stalwart this information. He is never to know about his brother.

Gerald Barter

Gerald Barter
Director, Global Protection Force

THINGS YOU'LL FIND IN EVERY BOOK

Watch Phone: The only gadget Jack wears all the time, even when he's not on official business. His Watch Phone is the central gadget that makes most others work. There are lots of important features, most importantly the "C" button, which reveals the code of the day – necessary to unlock Jack's Secret Agent Book Bag. There are buttons on both sides, one of which ejects his life-saving Melting Ink Pen. Beyond these functions, it also works as a phone and, of course, gives Jack the time of day.

Global Protection Force (GPF): The GPF is the organization Jack works for. It's a worldwide force of young secret agents whose aim is to protect the world's people, places and possessions. No one knows exactly where its main offices are located (all correspondence and gadgets for repair are sent to a special PO Box, and training is held at various locations around the world), but Jack thinks it's somewhere cold, like the Arctic Circle.

Whizzy: Jack's magical miniature globe. Almost every night at precisely 7:30 P.M., the GPF uses Whizzy to send Jack the identity of the country that he must travel to. Whizzy can't talk, but he can cough up messages. Jack's parents don't know Whizzy is anything more than a normal globe.

The Magic Map: The magical map hanging on Jack's bedroom wall. Unlike most maps, the GPF's map is made of a mysterious wood. Once Jack inserts the country piece from Whizzy, the map swallows Jack whole and sends him away on his missions. When he returns, he arrives precisely one minute after he left.

Secret Agent Book Bag: The Book Bag that Jack wears on every adventure. Licensed only to GPF secret agents, it contains top-secret gadgets necessary to foil bad guys and escape certain death. To activate the bag before each mission, Jack must punch in a secret code given to him by his Watch Phone. Once he's away, all he has to do is place his finger on the zip, which identifies him as the owner of the bag and immediately opens.

THE STALWART FAMILY

Jack's dad, John

He moved the family to England when Jack was two, in order to take a job with an aerospace company. As far as Jack knows, his dad designs and manufactures airplane parts. Jack's dad thinks he is an ordinary boy and that his other son, Max, attends a school in Switzerland. Jack's dad is American and his mum is British, which makes Jack a bit of both.

Jack's mum, Corinne

One of the greatest mums as far as Jack is concerned. When she and her husband received a letter from a posh school in Switzerland inviting Max to attend, they were overjoyed. Since Max left six months ago, they have received numerous notes in Max's handwriting telling them he's OK. Little do they know it's all a lie and that it's the GPF sending those letters.

Jack's older brother, Max

Two years ago, at the age of nine, Max joined the GPF. Max used to tell Jack about his adventures and show him how to work his secret-agent gadgets. When the family received a letter inviting Max to attend a school in Europe, Jack figured it was to do with the GPF. Max told him he was right, but that he couldn't tell Jack anything about why he was going away.

Nine-year-old Jack Stalwart

Four months ago, Jack received an anonymous note saying: "Your brother is in danger. Only you can save him." As soon as he could, Jack applied to be a secret agent too. Since that time, he's battled some of the world's most dangerous villains, and hopes some day in his travels to find and rescue his brother, Max.

DESTINATION:
China

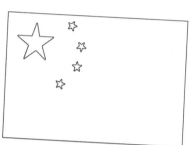

Most people make their living as farmers. They grow lots of things, including rice, corn, sweet potatoes and peanuts

☐

China is located on the continent of Asia

☐

Beijing (pronounced *bay-jing*) is its capital city

☐

It's the third largest country in the world. One out of every five people on Earth live in China

Chinese people use symbols instead of letters in their writing. There are over 40,000 Chinese symbols

☐

China's official currency is the Yuan

☐

Mandarin is the official language, although lots of other languages are spoken

GIANT PANDA: FACTS AND FIGURES

More Giant Pandas live in China than
anywhere else in the world

The Chinese name for the Giant Panda
means "large bear cat"

Pandas mainly eat bamboo, although they like
eggs, honey and insects too

Since their digestion is poor, they eat for up
to twelve hours a day

Panda paws have five fingers and one thumb

The main threat to the Giant Panda is the loss
of habitat due to logging and human
development

THE TERRACOTTA ARMY: FACTS AND FIGURES

The Terracotta Army is not a real army, but a collection of over 8,000 clay statues made to look like real officers and soldiers

They were commissioned by the first emperor of unified China, Qin Shi Huang, and placed near his tomb when he died in 210 BC

The statues were discovered in 1974 near Xi'an by a man drilling for water

The army is organized into three "pits": the main army, the military guard and the command unit

No two soldiers are the same. Each has a different face and uniform

The emperor's tomb itself remains sealed

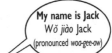

SECRET AGENT GADGET INSTRUCTION MANUAL

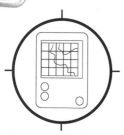

Map Mate: When you're lost or need to get somewhere fast, use the GPF's Map Mate. This clever gadget receives signals from satellites in space to give you a map of any city or town in the world. It can also show you how to get from one place to another using directional arrows to guide the way.

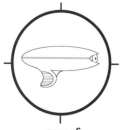

Laser Burst: The GPF's Laser Burst is a handheld laser that emits a powerful white light capable of slicing through almost anything. Perfect when you need to burn a quick hole, start a camp fire or cut through something hard.

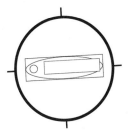

Secret Language Decoder: When you need to figure out what someone or something is saying, use the GPF's Secret Language Decoder. To decipher foreign text, push the "read" button. To translate speech, push "listen" and wait for the translation to appear on the screen.

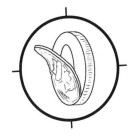

Motion Sensor: The GPF's Motion Sensor looks like a coin but it's actually a hi-tech motion-detecting device. Just peel off the fake backing to stick it in place. Once it's attached it will send a signal to your Watch Phone if anything moves within ten feet of its range.

Chapter 1:
The Throw

Jack and his mum drove into the village hall car park. "I'll pick you up in an hour," she said. Jack opened the door, quickly waved "goodbye" and shut the door behind him. His mum had some grocery shopping to do. She put the car in gear and pulled away.

Every weekend, twenty kids including Jack met to learn judo from Mr. Baskin, one of the best judo instructors in Great

Britain. Judo is a type of martial art from Japan. Thanks to Mr. Baskin, Jack had already earned his yellow belt. Not only was judo recommended by the GPF, it was something that Jack loved doing.

As he entered the building, he spotted his friends Richard and Charlie. They were also dressed in the judo uniform called a *judogi*. A *judogi* was a white jacket and

trousers with a special belt tied around the waist. Jack walked over to say "hi," but almost at the same time Mr. Baskin yelled out to the class.

"OK, everyone!" he said. "Let's begin."

Jack went over to the edge of the mat, tidied up his *judogi* and tossed off his flip-flops. Then he, Richard, Charlie and the rest of the class stepped onto the mat and waited for instructions.

"Floor work!" Mr. Baskin said. "Commando style!" he added.

Everyone knew what to do. Hurrying to one side of the mat, the first row of students dropped to the floor and lay on their stomachs. Then they used their elbows to pull themselves across the mat, like soldiers in a trench. Almost as soon as they'd finished, Mr. Baskin shouted another command.

"Cartwheels!" he said.

Jack could hear the rest of the boys sigh in dread. While the girls in the class loved doing cartwheels, it was difficult for Jack and the other boys to get their legs round.

Jack did his best, and when he'd made it across the mat, he heard Mr. Baskin call everyone back to the center. They returned to the middle, sat back on their heels and listened carefully to what the teacher had to say.

"Can anyone tell me what *hansoku-make* means?" he asked.

Jack knew the answer. He raised his hand. "Disqualification," he offered when Mr. Baskin called on him.

"Yes!" said Mr. Baskin, pleased that the first answer of the day was a correct one. "And what causes a disqualification?" he asked.

Charlie's hand shot up. "Putting your fingers up an opponent's sleeve," he answered.

"Well," said Mr. Baskin, "that wouldn't cause a *hansoku-make*. Can anyone tell me what putting your hands up an opponent's sleeve *would* cause?"

Richard raised his hand. "A *shido*?"

"Excellent!" Mr. Baskin said. "Yes, putting your fingers up someone's sleeve would cause a *shido*, or small penalty."

"What else?" he asked, searching for other means of disqualification.

A girl a few kids back from Jack raised her hand. Although Jack didn't know her name, he knew that she was more skilled than he was because she was wearing an orange belt.

"Punching someone in the face," she replied with a naughty smile.

The instructor smiled back. "Good one, Charlotte," he said. "Any other ideas?"

Charlie raised his hand again. "What about if you wear metal or jewelry?" he asked.

"Yes!" said Mr. Baskin, excited that his class had been paying attention to previous lessons.

Another girl raised her hand too. Jack recognized her as Emma, a girl who lived a few streets over from him. She was eight years old.

"Biting someone?" she offered.

"Excellent," said Mr. Baskin. "All of those things – punching, wearing metal and biting – can lead to disqualification.

"Now," he continued, moving on from the questions and answers, "today, we're going to learn a new throw. It's called a *harai goshi*. It's known as the "sweeping hip throw" and is an excellent move that can have a number of results."

He got up and, with the help of Tim, a thirteen-year-old boy who sometimes assisted him, showed the class how it was done. When the demonstration was over, the instructor told everyone to find a partner. Richard and Charlie nabbed each other first, which left Jack alone, but not for long. Charlotte, the girl with the orange belt, turned up in front of him almost instantly.

"Wanna be my partner?" she asked.

Jack looked around for another partner, but everyone had already paired up. He never liked practicing with girls. He didn't like the thought of hurting them.

"OK," he said reluctantly. "Shall we get started?"

Jack and Charlotte bowed to each other. As Jack reached for Charlotte's sleeve, she

moved quickly. She grabbed his right arm,
twisted in toward his body, lifted him up
on her back, then grabbed his trouser leg
and threw him on the floor.

THWACK!

Jack's body hit the mat hard. He'd never been thrown by a girl before. He looked up at Charlotte, who was standing above him, arms crossed, with one of those know-it-all grins on her face. Hopefully his friends hadn't seen what happened.

Pretending that it didn't bother him, Jack got up and coolly said, "I let you do that."

He and Charlotte faced each other for another match. As they tidied their *judogis*, Jack was going through the moves in his head. Just as they were about to begin, Mr. Baskin shouted for everyone to find a new partner. Without saying a word, Charlotte flicked her ponytail and strutted off with her nose in the air.

Before Jack could think about getting back at Charlotte, Adam stepped in front

of him. He and Adam were in the same
class at school. The two of them bowed to
each other, and after a pretty good
wrestle, Jack threw Adam to the floor.
Then they repeated the move and Jack let
Adam do the same to him.

They practiced over and over, so that by the end of that session, Jack was pretty good at performing the *harai goshi*. Now all he had to do was find Charlotte again. He'd throw *her* this time round. But unfortunately that wasn't going to happen – at least, not today.

"Gather up!" yelled Mr. Baskin, motioning for everyone to sit in front of him in a row.

Jack and the rest of the students sat on their heels across from Mr. Baskin, who congratulated them on their hard work. As soon as they were dismissed, Jack, Richard and Charlie gathered up their things and walked outside.

While they were waiting for their mums, they talked about lots of things, like whether they were going to enter the next judo competition. (Richard was, Charlie wasn't and Jack thought he might.)

When Jack's mum pulled up, Jack said goodbye to his friends and climbed into the car which was filled with groceries.

When he got home, he helped his mum put away the food and then played a car-racing game on his Xbox. Sometime after dinner, he kissed his mum good-night – his dad was working all weekend again – and made his way upstairs to his room.

As he got to his door, Jack flipped the sign outside to "KEEP OUT." Although he loved his mum, he didn't want her just barging in. After all, top-secret stuff happened in there. And it was nearly 7:30 P.M.

Chapter 2:
The Deer-Shaped
Country

As soon as Jack shut the door, he looked
over at his miniature globe, Whizzy, who
was fast asleep. For some reason, seeing
Whizzy like this made Jack think about
the time they first met. It was at the GPF
swearing-in ceremony, when Jack officially
became a secret agent.

Ms. Pembroke, the lady in charge of
globe selection, told Jack to pick one from
a long table of globes. As Jack walked by,
he noticed that each had a name like

"Zippy" or "Zoom." When he came to a little globe called "Whizzy," he stopped and leaned in for a closer look.

As he did so, the globe smiled, lifted his eyebrows and winked at Jack. Thinking he was cute, Jack picked him up and turned to Ms. Pembroke. "I'll have this one," he said. And that's how Whizzy came to be in Jack's house that night.

Jack walked over to his friend, just as the time on his Watch Phone ticked over to 7:30 P.M. Almost instantly, Whizzy's eyes popped open. When he saw Jack, he winked and began to spin.

Jack watched as the globe twirled even faster. After a few seconds, Whizzy coughed. *Ahem!* A jigsaw piece in the shape of a country flew out of his mouth. Jack rushed over to pick it up. Whizzy, exhausted from the exercise, fell asleep again.

This one looks like a deer with two antlers, thought Jack as he studied the piece in his hand. Now, let's see where it fits.

Jack carried the piece over to his Magic Map. The Magic Map on his bedroom wall had over 150 countries carved into its special wood. When Jack put the jigsaw piece from Whizzy's mouth in the right spot, the Magic Map transported him to his next mission.

Starting in the upper left corner of the map, Jack slid the piece over every lump and bump. When he crossed over the continent of Europe and passed into the continent of Asia, the piece snapped into place. The word "CHINA" appeared, then quickly vanished.

"I can't believe it," said Jack. "I'm going to China!" Ever since he and his parents started eating at the local Chinese restaurant, Jack had been interested in the food and language of that country.

Knowing that many people in China didn't speak English, Jack figured he needed his Secret Language Decoder. Punching the "C" button on his Watch Phone, he called up the code of the day.

After receiving the word D-U-M-P-L-I-N-G, he typed it into the lock on his special Book Bag and waited for it to snap open. When it did, he checked the contents inside. Sure enough, his Secret Language Decoder was there, as were his Magic Key Maker, Motion Sensor and Net Tosser.

Closing his bag, Jack slipped his arms through the straps and tightened them over his shoulders. Standing before the Magic Map, he looked at the country of China.

Inside, a small orange light began to glow. It grew until it lit up his entire room.

When the time was right, Jack yelled, "Off to China!" Then the light flickered and burst, and swallowed him into the Magic Map.

Chapter 3:
The Misty Forest

When Jack opened his eyes, he found himself standing in the middle of a big forest covered in mist and filled with tall stalks of green bamboo. Jack knew that bamboo was a type of grass, not a tree, and that it grew in most parts of Asia.

In his GPF training, he'd learned about the wonders of bamboo. It was light yet strong enough to make lots of things, including rafts (it could float) and ladders.

Inside the stalk were tiny worms that could be eaten if you needed food.

Jack had tasted a bamboo worm once. Surprisingly, it didn't taste like a worm, but like peanut butter, one of Jack's favorite foods. Knowing about bamboo was an important skill if you were on assignment in Asia.

As Jack's mind drifted off thinking about the grass, the sound of cracking branches from behind brought things back into focus. Jack quickly turned round to find a small woman dressed in khaki-colored clothing walking towards him. She looked friendly enough; her eyes were as gentle as her smile.

"*Nǐ hào*," she said as she approached Jack. "*Wǒ jiào* Mei. It is a pleasure to meet you," and she bowed her head in Jack's direction.

Guessing she was his contact, Jack

bowed his head in respect. "*Wǒ jiào* Jack," he replied. He decided to see if Mei spoke English. "It's a pleasure to meet you too. What can I do for you?"

She nodded to show she understood him. "A terrible thing has happened," said Mei, lowering her eyes and shaking her head. "You are standing in the Wolong Nature Reserve, one of the largest habitats for the endangered Giant Panda. There are only about a thousand Giant Pandas left in the world, and many of them live here in the reserve.

"Last night," she carried on, "one of our female pandas, Ling, disappeared. No one knows what happened to her, but I think she was kidnapped. I need you to find Ling and bring her back to the reserve as soon as possible."

Before Jack could respond, Mei added, "Time is especially important, as Ling needs bamboo to survive. The longer she is away from the reserve and her bamboo, the more her life is in danger."

"Don't worry," said Jack, trying to reassure Mei. "I'll find Ling and bring her back to you. The first thing I need to do is take a look at where she was last seen."

"No problem," answered Mei. "I will ask Fong, one of our park assistants, to show you around. He should be able to help, since he was assigned to Ling and kept a record of her daily habits."

"Terrific," said Jack, who was anxious to start his mission. "I would love to meet him."

Chapter 4:
The Hairy Teenager

Mei radioed for Fong to come and join them. Within minutes, the park assistant appeared. When he did, Jack was a bit surprised. He didn't look anything like what he'd expected.

Firstly, Fong wasn't an adult; he was only a teenager. Secondly, he was dressed completely in black. His hair looked like it hadn't been washed in ages and he had a tattoo of a scorpion on the back of his left hand. Out of a mole on his chin grew a

curly black hair that was so long, Jack
couldn't stop staring at it.

"What are you looking at?" Fong growled.
Jack was surprised that he could speak
English.

"Uh . . . Nothing," said Jack, snapping himself out of it. He quickly extended his hand to Fong. "Hi, I am here to help find Ling."

Fong glared at Jack, probably still annoyed that he'd been staring at his mole. He didn't put out his hand to shake Jack's.

"Fong," said Mei, interrupting the uncomfortable pause, "why don't you show Jack where Ling was last seen?"

"It would be great if you could," said Jack. "There might be something there that would be useful to the investigation."

For a second Fong stared at Jack. Then he turned his back on him and started walking into the forest.

"You will have to excuse Fong," said Mei. "He's a bit shy. He doesn't really say that much. And of course he is worried about Ling."

"That's all right, Mei," said Jack politely. "I meet all kinds of people in this job. I am sure that Fong and I will get along great." As he waved goodbye he added, "Next time I see you, I will have Ling with me."

"I hope so," said Mei, and she waved back.

Chapter 5:
The Dirt Road

"So what made you decide to be a park assistant?" Jack asked Fong, trying to make conversation as they trudged through the forest, stepping over fallen branches along the way.

Fong rolled his eyes and continued to walk ahead of Jack. For every step that Fong took, Jack had to take two.

"I mean," Jack carried on, "it must be exciting to see the Giant Panda in the wild. I've only ever seen one in a picture or on the Internet. What are they like in real life?"

Fong continued to ignore Jack. It was obvious that he was still upset about his mole. "Well, I am sure it won't take long to find Ling," said Jack as they carried on.

Just then, Fong stopped and turned to look at Jack. He stared at him for a few seconds and then pointed to a clearing in the forest. "Over there," he muttered.

"Great!" said Jack as he rushed toward the clearing.

It was a large area that had been flattened by the weight of the panda as she was sitting, probably eating bamboo. Around the clearing were broken bits of bamboo grass and fresh animal droppings.

When Jack bent down for a closer look, he didn't notice anything unusual about the bamboo or the poo. But he did see a

path of broken twigs and trodden-on
grass leading from the clearing and to the
right. Perhaps they drugged and then
dragged Ling from this spot, Jack thought.
He followed the trail with his eyes and
saw that it went under some trees.

"Where does that lead?" Jack asked
Fong. Fong raised his eyebrow, shrugged
his shoulders and shook his head as if to
say "I don't know."

Motioning for Fong to follow him, Jack quickly but carefully made his way into the woods. As he pushed some hanging branches out of his way, he spied some light peeking through. It was only about ten yards away. There must be another way out, he thought.

Studying the ground as he walked, Jack spotted a square piece of paper. He bent down to pick it up. What he originally thought was a piece of paper was actually a book of matches. Odd, he thought, that something like this would be lying in the middle of the forest.

Since he didn't have time to decipher the Chinese characters that were printed on the outside, he tucked it into his trouser pocket and carried on. For all Jack knew, Ling could still be nearby. He needed to hurry.

The forest stopped at a dirt track that was covered in tire marks. It looked as though one set had been made recently. To the right, the road ended; to the left, it carried on north. Although the tire marks in the dirt were fuzzy, Jack had a pretty good idea that the vehicle was some kind of truck.

Jack turned to Fong. "Whoever took Ling must have loaded her into a truck here," he explained. "We need to drive north to see if we can pick up any more clues."

Fong looked at Jack and then picked up his mobile phone. "I'll call a friend," he muttered. He dialled a number and spoke to someone in Chinese. After only ten minutes, a truck pulled up in front of Jack and Fong. The passenger door opened and Jack looked in.

Sitting in the driver's seat was another dark-haired teenage park assistant. He grinned at Jack.

"Hey there," he said, flashing his teeth. "I'm Wong. I hear you're looking for Ling. Climb in and we can all look together."

"Great!" said Jack, pleased that someone else was as interested as he was in finding the panda.

Jack crawled into the back of the truck, while Fong climbed into the front next to Wong. The next thing Jack knew, Wong slammed his foot on the accelerator and the three of them took off, leaving only a flurry of dust circling behind them.

Chapter 6:
The Secret Language

Within minutes of them driving down the dirt road, Fong reached into a compartment in the dashboard and pulled out a packet of cigarettes. He then pulled a book of matches from his shirt pocket and lit a cigarette.

After taking a long, extended puff, Fong rolled down the window and tossed the empty matchbook out. But the wind from the speeding truck sent the matchbook flying into the back and onto Jack's lap.

He picked it up and passed it over the front seat to Fong.

"Excuse me, Fong," he said. "This blew back inside."

"Give me that!" Fong snapped as he turned round and grabbed it from Jack. "Keep your hands off my things."

Jack sat back in his seat, in a state of shock. Why was Fong being so nasty? He knew that Fong had been upset about him staring at his mole, but this was taking things a bit too far. To make matters worse, Wong began to laugh at what Fong had said, and the two of them were now sniggering together.

Jack was starting to feel uncomfortable. Maybe he shouldn't have taken a ride with Wong and Fong after all. The only reason he did so was because he thought Fong might be useful in gathering information about the panda. Now the two teenagers were talking to each other in Chinese, and Wong was looking at Jack in the rear-view mirror with a nasty expression on his face.

There was only one thing to do, and that was to figure out what these guys were saying. Quietly, Jack opened his Book Bag and pulled out his Secret Language Decoder. This gadget could not only listen in on conversations and translate what someone was saying into

English, it could also read foreign text. It was one of the GPF's most useful tools.

When Jack pushed the black button on the top of the silver box, a short wire with a microphone on the end popped out. He pushed some buttons which told the box to listen in on what Fong and Wong were saying and translate it from Chinese into English. As the Decoder listened, Jack watched the illuminated screen in the middle.

"We need to get rid of him," Fong said, taking a long drag on his cigarette. "He's smarter than I thought. He figured out the panda was taken out of the park and loaded onto a truck. It's only a matter of time before he realizes it was this one."

When Jack heard that, his eyes bulged. He knew there was something odd about Fong and Wong, but he would never have guessed they were involved in taking Ling.

"I agree. Let's kill him." Wong laughed.

Jack gulped.

"We can tell him we're taking him north through the park to the Great Wall," suggested Fong. "We can say that there is someone there who knows something about the panda."

"Perfect," said Wong. "I like your plan."

Although Jack hadn't noticed it before, he realized as he watched Wong drive that he had the same scorpion tattoo as Fong on his left hand. Fong turned round to talk to Jack as Wong continued to drive north through the reserve. Jack quickly moved the Secret Language Decoder out of the way.

"We're going to take a little drive," he said to Jack, "out of the park and towards the Great Wall of China. Wong says that there is someone on the way who knows about the panda. I think we should check it out."

"Sure, Fong," said Jack calmly,

pretending to go along with the plan. "I'd love to meet the contact."

Fong turned back round in his seat with a sly smile on his face. Jack looked through the window. They passed a sign which read:

YOU ARE NOW
LEAVING
THE WOLONG
NATURE
RESERVE

HAVE A NICE DAY

Jack laid the Secret Language Decoder on the seat next to him and closed his eyes. He couldn't believe this was happening. He was being hijacked by two criminals who wanted him dead. He

needed to escape from Fong and Wong
before they got to the Great Wall.

But how was Jack going to get away
from two people who were stronger than
he was, and from a truck that was traveling
at fifty miles per hour? He needed to be
patient. Jack was going to have to wait for
an opportunity. He just hoped that break
would come soon.

Chapter 7:
The Opportunity

Fong, Wong and Jack traveled for a while when, out of the blue, Jack spotted another sign. It read:

WORLD FAMOUS
TERRACOTTA
ARMY
5 MILES AHEAD

That's it! thought Jack. Just the other week, he had seen a television program about the Terracotta Army. He knew that nearly 8,000 clay figurines made up the army and were housed in a giant museum. A perfect place to try and lose these guys, he thought.

"I've never seen the Terracotta Army before," said Jack. "Can we stop so that I can take a look?"

Fong looked at Wong, surprised at Jack's interest. But since Fong didn't know Jack had translated their conversation, he thought it was just an honest kid's strange request.

"Yeah, sure," Fong said. "We can stop for five minutes so you can see a few clay people."

Within minutes, they'd arrived at the complex. The museum building was huge, as was the car park. After pulling in, Wong found a parking place and turned off the engine. Fong got out of the truck and pushed his seat forward to let Jack out.

"Now don't go too far, young man," said Wong.

"Don't worry. I won't!" said Jack, strapping on his Book Bag and walking toward the main building.

But as he approached the front doors, something made Jack stop. He had the feeling that he'd forgotten something. He turned toward the truck and spotted Fong reaching into the back seat. He pulled something out and showed it to Wong. When Jack realized what it was, he panicked. It was his Secret Language Decoder.

Not only was he going to get a telling off from the GPF, it also looked like Jack was going to be in trouble with Fong and Wong. At first, the two teenagers didn't know what the strange box was, but as soon as they saw the English words on the screen, they worked it out. Jack could tell they weren't happy.

As Jack watched, Fong turned to face him. When their eyes met, Fong lifted his fists and shook them at Jack. Then the two park assistants started to run in Jack's direction.

Quickly, Jack dashed through the front doors and into the museum. Above him were several signs. One of them said "PIT 1." Thinking he didn't have time to be choosy, he followed the arrows. Before he knew it, he was standing on an elevated viewing platform in a massive, vaulted room.

The walkway he was standing on traveled in a square around the site, so that people could see the army from every angle. On the floor was the main army itself – 6,000 of the terracotta soldiers. As Jack stood there, wondering what to do, he heard Fong and Wong burst into the complex.

"We're going to get you, kid!" screamed Fong.

"You can't hide from us!" yelled Wong.

Jack had to act fast. The only way out of this was to go down into the pit itself, and try to lose them among the terra-cotta statues. Jack quickly lowered himself down. When he looked up, he found himself surrounded by some of the fiercest figures he'd ever seen.

Jack darted through the sculptures, trying to zigzag in a way that would confuse Fong and Wong. But from the elevated platform

where they were standing, the two teenage boys could see everything. They soon lowered themselves down and continued the chase.

Jack stopped for a second to see where they were. Fong and Wong were only a few soldiers behind. He carried on moving as quickly as he could. When he reached

the end of that section of soldiers, he
looked up. Above him was another
viewing platform.

He leaped up to the lower bar and
pulled himself onto the top of the stand.
Giving himself a moment to catch his
breath, Jack looked around for Fong
and Wong. They were just below him,

trying to pull themselves up onto the walkway too.

Jack sprinted across the platform and through the door marked "EXIT," not stopping until he reached Fong and Wong's truck. Luckily for him they hadn't locked it, so it was easy to grab his Secret Language Decoder.

With the gadget tucked safely back into his Book Bag, Jack looked for a way to escape. Unfortunately he was too young to drive.

Just then, he spied a tour bus parked
across from where he was standing.
Thankfully the door of the bus was wide
open.

Perfect, thought Jack.

He made a break for it, sprinting and
diving through the open bus door, just
as Fong and Wong burst out from the
museum. Lying on the floor of the bus,
Jack grabbed onto the handle that closed
the door and, with one yank, sealed it
shut.

Crawling commando-style along the
floor down the middle of the bus, he
found a hidden spot near the back. He
lifted his head just enough to see Fong
and Wong standing in the middle of the
car park. They looked confused. No
wonder – Jack was nowhere in sight.

He ducked and hid in the back for what
seemed like an eternity, until he heard

a big gush of air. It was the door to the bus – someone had opened it. Grabbing onto the straps of his Book Bag, he waited quietly in case it was Fong and Wong.

"Welcome aboard, ladies and gentlemen," bellowed an American voice from the front as people started piling aboard the bus. "I hope that you have enjoyed your tour of the Terracotta Army. Next stop is the Great Wall of China," it went on, "and the magnificent capital city of Beijing."

Must be the bus driver, thought Jack. He stayed hidden in the back, so the driver wouldn't know he was there. As the tourists shuffled around and found a seat on the bus, Jack risked another look at the car park. There was no sign of Fong, Wong or their truck anywhere.

Although Jack didn't want to travel all the way to Beijing, he knew that this bus was the safest place to be. There wasn't any sign of the two teenagers in the car park, but that didn't mean they weren't lurking, lying in wait for him somewhere on the main road. He settled himself in for the journey and began to think about what to do next.

He still had to find and rescue Ling, capture Fong and Wong and return the panda to the reserve. He wondered where those nasty teens were, and where they'd stashed Ling. Jack had a lot of thinking and planning to do. Time was running out.

Chapter 8:
The Great Wall

Jack took his Encryption Notebook out, activated it with his thumb and began to jot down some thoughts with its pen. The GPF's Encryption Notebook cleverly allowed secret agents to take notes and then turn their words into code, so criminals couldn't use the information if they got their hands on the gadget. Jack wrote down what had happened and the things he noticed:

Suspects: Fong and Wong; last names unknown.

Suspect profile: Both about sixteen years old. Smokers. Both like to wear dark clothes.

Distinguishing marks: Both have scorpion tattoo on left hand. Fong has hairy mole on his chin.

Other information: Home addresses unknown.

As Jack reviewed the information, something became clear. Fong and Wong had to be part of a gang. Not only did they dress alike, they also had the same scorpion tattoo.

Gang members often tattooed themselves to show their support for each other. The fact that they both had the same tattoo was no coincidence, thought Jack. But he still wasn't sure what the gang was all about and why the two boys had stolen Ling.

One thing was for sure, and that was that Fong and Wong liked to smoke. Although smoking was a bad habit, it wasn't an odd thing to do. This made Jack remember the matchbook he'd found in the forest near where Ling was last seen. He pulled it out of his trouser pocket and looked at it closely.

It looked identical to the matchbook that Fong had tried to toss out of the truck's window – the one that flew back at Jack. The color was the same, as was the placement of the Chinese characters on the front.

Since people often took matchbooks from whatever bar or restaurant was

offering them, Jack wondered if the one in the forest also belonged to Fong. If Jack could decipher the Chinese writing, it should tell him where Fong collected it. Then Jack could visit the place and see if it was where the two teens hung out.

As Jack carried on writing and thinking, the tour bus drove through the craggy mountains of China toward the Great Wall. In the distance, he could see the huge structure. It took over one million

people to build it and many of them lost their lives. As Jack looked at the wall, which looked like the ridged back of a sleeping dragon, he thought about what it would have been like to live in ancient China.

Even though they were now hundreds of miles away from the Terracotta Army, Jack kept a lookout for Fong and Wong through the back window. You could never tell when and where your enemy would surface.

Chapter 9:
The Clue

Placing the matchbook on the pull-down table in front of his seat, Jack grabbed his Secret Language Decoder again. Pushing the black button, he made the microphone disappear back inside. After switching it from "listen" to "read" mode, he waved the other end of the box over the Chinese writing on the matchbook. The Secret Language Decoder took the information and translated it into English for Jack on the screen. It said:

Happy Valley Restaurant

in the heart of Beijing. Delicious food at delicious prices. Dazhalan Lu Lane.

Phone: 66013269.

"Interesting," muttered Jack. Fong had picked up this matchbook at a restaurant in the Chinese capital of Beijing. But why were they in Beijing? Perhaps, Jack reckoned, that was where they had the base for their operations. Deciding it might be a promising tip, Jack decided to stay on the bus all the way to the capital city.

Who knows – this could be my lucky break, he thought.

Chapter 10:
The Scorpion

After hours of dozing on and off, Jack finally woke up to the loud voice of the American bus driver.

"Here we are, ladies and gentlemen," he said. "The capital city of China, Beijing. Our first stop is Tian'anmen Square. You have two hours to tour the square and the Forbidden City before meeting back here."

As the paying passengers made their way off the bus, Jack joined them and did his best to blend in. Luckily for him,

the bus driver was too busy making
notes on his clipboard to notice Jack as
he walked by.

Stepping out of the vehicle, Jack made
his way over to the great square.
Tian'anmen Square is the largest square
in the world, well known as the entrance
to the Forbidden City and as the site of a
famous student protest in 1989.

He found a metal bench not too far away
and sat down. Having made a mental note
of the restaurant's address, he pulled out
the GPF's Map Mate. The Map Mate could
download satellite images of any neigh-
borhood in the world, and give you
detailed maps of how to get from one
place to the next.

After Jack had punched in the address, Dazhalan Lu Lane, and his starting point, Tian'anmen Square, the Map Mate created a map of his exact route. It not only listed the streets in Chinese and English, but also used arrows to show him the quickest way of getting there.

With his Map Mate in hand, Jack stood up and headed south. He walked through the plaza, under an enormous gate and onto an extremely busy road with chemists, clothing and snack shops everywhere.

After a few blocks, he turned right onto a very old and narrow road with medicine and clothing stores housed in ancient buildings. On the street itself were several vendors selling everything from Chinese dumplings and eggs to cheese and fizzy drinks.

Jack carried on along three more streets and found himself on Dazhalan Lu Lane. According to the matchbook, this was where he would find Happy Valley restaurant. Almost as soon as he started looking, he spied the place. It was the only restaurant on the lane and had pretty red Chinese lanterns hanging outside.

But as Jack approached, something else caught his eye. Next to the restaurant was a building with an interesting front window. Painted on it was a gigantic scorpion, just like the one on Fong and Wong's left hand.

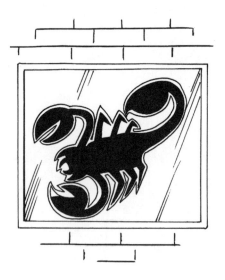

Now things were starting to make sense. If Jack was right, this was the Scorpion Gang's headquarters. And the only way to find out what was truly going on was to get inside.

Chapter 11:
The Headquarters

Keeping an eye out for Fong and Wong, Jack peered through the window. It was completely dark inside. It didn't look as though anyone was there.

Trying not to draw attention to himself, Jack slipped his hand over the door knob. He gave it a yank, but it was locked. Reaching into his Book Bag, he pulled out the GPF's Magic Key Maker. After Jack had slid the rubber tube into the key hole, it instantly hardened, forming a key. He looked over his shoulder for any passers-by, before turning the special key and stepping inside.

Once in, he closed the door behind him and pulled what looked like a round coin out of his shirt pocket. The coin wasn't actually a coin, but a GPF Motion Sensor that would send a signal to his Watch Phone if Fong, Wong or the other gang members returned. As he was attaching the Motion Sensor to the bottom corner of the door, he heard a noise that made him jump.

"*KACK! SQUAWK!*"

He turned round and listened again for the noise.

"*KACK! SQUAWK!*"

There it was. There was only one thing that could make that kind of sound, thought Jack, and that was a bird. He peered through the darkness and saw the eyes of a bird locked in a cage.

"I don't suppose you know what Fong and Wong are up to?" he whispered to

the bird, half-jokingly, as he walked up to
the cage to have a better look.

"*KACK! KACK!*" replied the bird as it
flapped its wings.

Jack made his way round it and passed
several other crates and coops with
strange animals inside. Although he
didn't recognize the first bird, he knew

some of these creatures. One was a
golden monkey, a rare breed found only
in China. In a large wooden crate there
was a snow leopard that looked as if it
had been drugged. Finally, and most
surprisingly, there was a Crested Ibis,
one of the rarest birds in the entire
world.

Having seen these animals in their cages, Jack realized what Fong and Wong were up to. They were stealing endangered animals and selling them. That would explain why they took Ling. Since the panda would have been too big for this room, Jack reckoned she was on another level. But where? He needed to press on and look for more clues.

As Jack walked through the large room, he came to a flight of stairs. He grabbed onto the railing and climbed, taking each step slowly so the stairs wouldn't squeak.

When he reached the top of the first flight, he peered down the dark corridor to his right. At the end of the hallway he could see a small room with a television flickering. Dozing in wooden chairs in front of the TV were two teenage boys – no doubt other members of the Scorpion Gang.

Carefully climbing to the next level, Jack

found himself facing a door. Rather than
open it and risk waking the boys below,
he pulled out the GPF's Ear Amp. He
clipped the tiny device into his ear and
listened closely for any noise on the other
side. There were several things.

The first sound was of the traffic in the street below. The second was the sound of rustling grass. Finally, he could hear something chomping on food. Putting these three things together, Jack worked out that there was a rooftop terrace through the door and Ling, the Giant Panda, was probably out there eating bamboo.

Jack was facing a pretty risky situation. Somehow he had to rescue the panda without waking the boys below. He took a few moments to think of a plan and then moved toward the door to put it in motion.

Chapter 12:
The Intruders

But just as Jack was about to open the door, the Motion Sensor alarm on his Watch Phone went off. He looked down the stairs and saw the lights flicker on. Someone had entered the building. A male voice began speaking in Chinese. Jack pulled his Secret Language Decoder out of his bag.

"Get up!" said the first voice. It didn't sound like an adult's. It came from a teenager.

"Wake up, you lazy lot!" A second teenage voice rang out. Jack recognized it as Fong's, which meant the first voice he'd heard was probably Wong's.

From where he was, Jack could hear the boys on the first level get out of their chairs. He then saw them shuffle down the steps to the ground floor, where they greeted Fong and Wong.

Fong was acting like the leader of the group, telling everyone to move the animals to a new location. Jack heard the sound of cages scraping on the floor. Then he heard the front door slam shut. The other two boys must have left the building, thought Jack, because the only voices left were those of Fong and Wong.

Knowing that Ling was probably next, Jack realized he had to get moving. Quickly, he opened the door to the roof.

Unfortunately, as it opened, it made a

horrible sound that could be heard throughout the building.

SHREEEEEEEEK!

"Who's there?" shouted Fong as he raced up the stairs in time to see Jack step out onto the roof.

"Get him!" shouted Wong as they sprinted after him.

Chapter 13:
The Preparation

Jack stepped onto the terrace and scanned the roof. He needed to find a way to block the door.

To his left was a statue of Buddha, a man who was an important religious figure in China. The statue was heavy, so Jack slid it in front of the wooden door. That should hold for a few minutes, he thought, as he heard Fong and Wong slam into the door.

BLAM!

The Buddha statue barely moved.

BLAM!

It inched forward just a bit.

Jack's clever doorstop was only going to

last a little while. He needed to get to

Ling before Fong and Wong broke the door down.

The roof terrace was filled with pots of bamboo. Guessing the panda was hidden somewhere behind them, Jack hurried over. He pushed the grass aside, calling Ling's name as he searched. Finally he spied her, sitting quietly eating her food.

"Don't worry," he said, hoping she might understand. "I'll save you, and take you back home to Mei."

BLAM!

Jack looked over at the door. The statue wouldn't hold it closed for much longer. With one more push, Fong and Wong would be on the roof.

"Let's get going," said Jack to Ling as he reached into his Book Bag. He pulled out the bits to the Heli-Spacer. The GPF's Heli-Spacer was a disc that secret agents could stand on and fly using only their hands.

Quickly, Jack assembled the gadget. He took out the disc and opened it wide enough so that both he and Ling could fit on. Then he took a steel rod called the "prop" and snapped it into a hole on the disc. When he was ready, he pushed a button and two propellers shot out of the top of the "prop."

Leaving the Heli-Spacer behind, Jack dashed over to the pots of bamboo. He pulled out the GPF's Laser Burst and flicked it on. A bright white beam shot out through the tip. As Jack swiped it across the stalks, the bamboo quickly fell to the ground. Gathering as much as he could carry, he raced back to the Heli-Spacer, tying the stalks to the propeller with the belt from his trousers.

When Ling saw her bamboo, she

shuffled over and sat down on the disc. It was exactly the result that Jack was hoping for. He hooked a special rope around Ling and clipped it to the Heli-Spacer so she wouldn't fall off.

BLAM!

Jack spun his head round. The door to the roof came crashing open. Fong and Wong were standing in the doorway fuming with anger. For a second they couldn't work out what was going on, but when they realized what Jack was doing, they hurried after him.

Chapter 14:
The Technique

Jack dived onto the Heli-Spacer and clipped a special belt around his waist. He pulled himself up and thrust his arms forward as quickly as he could. The gadget began to lift off the ground, but not fast enough.

Fong and Wong grabbed onto Jack's ankles and reached up to unclip his belt. When Jack was no longer attached, they threw him violently onto the roof. He tumbled over a few times, coming to a stop on his back. With Jack no longer standing on the disc to drive it, the Heli-Spacer lowered itself and Ling back onto the roof.

"I'm going to get you, you punk!" shouted Fong as he glared at Jack.

"We'll show you who's boss!" snarled Wong, rubbing his fists together as though he was about to punch Jack.

The GPF always taught its secret agents to keep their cool in dangerous situations. Jack wasn't going to let these guys scare him. He crawled into a standing position.

"What do you say we finally finish this kid off?" said Wong.

"Be my guest," replied Fong, getting ready for a fight.

As Wong reached out to grab him, Jack remembered the *harai goshi*. Since the boys were Chinese, Jack reckoned they probably hadn't practiced this Japanese martial-art move before. He grabbed Wong's sleeves and moved in toward his body. Before Wong knew what was happening, Jack lifted him up on his

back, grabbed his trouser leg and tossed
him on the floor. As he went down,
Wong banged his head on one of the
bamboo pots, which knocked him out.

"Look what you did to my friend!" Fong
yelled. "I'll show you!" He took a knife
out of his pocket, flicked the blade and
lunged toward Jack.

But Jack was too quick. As Fong moved in, Jack grabbed his sleeves and swept his left leg across Fong's right foot. Fong started to fall, and Jack used his body weight to throw him onto his back. This was the *deashi harai*, or "forward foot sweep." It was one of Jack's favorite judo techniques. As Fong lay there, Jack stepped over him and stomped on his wrist, causing him to let go of the knife.

"Owww!" Fong yelled in pain, clutching his wrist with his other hand.

Jack picked up the knife, closed the blade and put it into his pocket for safe-keeping. Reaching into his Book Bag for his Net Tosser, he threw the expanding net on top of the two, trapping them underneath.

Jack phoned the local police and told

them what happened. He asked them to meet him there on the roof. By the time he'd finished on the phone, Wong had begun to wake up and Fong was crawling to his knees.

Within minutes, the police stormed the building. When they saw Ling on the roof, they frowned at Fong and Wong. Jack removed the Net Tosser so the police could handcuff the two thieves and take them away. As they were shoved toward the door, Fong and Wong looked back at Jack and sneered.

They were going away for a long time, thought Jack as he smugly waved good-bye to the duo. Harming or stealing a Giant Panda was a very bad thing to do.

A Chinese police officer came up the stairs toward Jack. He let him know that they'd caught the other two boys loading crates of animals onto a truck from another building a few blocks away. Jack was delighted – the Scorpion Gang had been stopped for good.

Chapter 15:
The Wrap-Up

Rather than fly Ling back to the nature reserve, Jack figured it would be better for the panda if a van took her home. Once he'd arranged it with the police and the local animal-protection unit, he called the Wolong Nature Reserve on his Watch Phone to tell Mei the good news. He could hear her voice through the tiny speaker.

"I can't thank you enough, Secret Agent Jack, for finding Ling," said Mei. "Who was responsible for taking her?"

"I'm sorry to tell you, but it was your park assistant Fong and his friend Wong," said Jack. He heard her gasp.

"They weren't exactly who they said they were," he explained. "They and two other boys were members of a gang that stole many animals. They were planning to sell them, and were holding them in a building here in Beijing. My bet," Jack added, "is that Fong worked at the reserve just to be able to take Ling."

Jack could hear the disappointment in Mei's voice. "That's terrible," she said. "I can't believe it."

"Me neither, Mei," said Jack. He glanced at the time. "Well, since everything is wrapped up, I'd better sign off."

"All right," said Mei. "You know you're welcome in China whenever you want to come back. And thank you again."

"No worries," replied Jack. "I hope Ling

is safe from now on." After saying goodbye, he punched a button on his phone
and hung up.

Jack scanned the roof. The crooks were gone, the police were gone and Ling was gone. He was the only one left. He punched a few buttons on his Watch Phone and when the time was right, yelled, "Off to England!"

Almost immediately, Jack was catapulted back home. When he arrived, he looked over at Whizzy (who was still dozing) and at his shelf in the far corner of his room. Sitting on top were trophies and framed photos from his first year of judo with Mr. Baskin.

Seeing these made him smile. It wasn't a gadget that had got him out of that situation with Fong and Wong – it was his quick-thinking and judo moves. Silently, he thanked Mr. Baskin for being such a good teacher.

As he changed his clothes and climbed into bed, Jack thought briefly about

Charlotte, the girl who threw him to the floor doing the *harai goshi*. Little did she know he'd had some extra practice. He'd definitely be ready to face-off again next weekend. In fact, he couldn't wait.

Peril at the Grand Prix: ITALY

BOOK (8)

Peril
at the
Grand Prix:
ITALY

Elizabeth Singer Hunt

Illustrated by Brian Williamson

WEINSTEIN BOOKS

ISBN: 978-1-60286-019-3

First Edition
10   9   8   7   6   5

*For Morgan, who
loves cars "so, so much"*

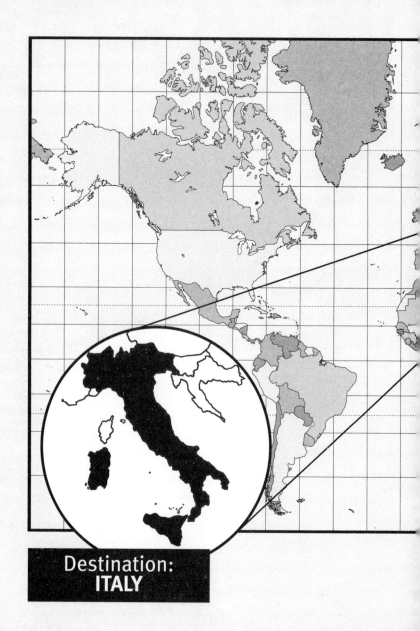

Destination:
ITALY

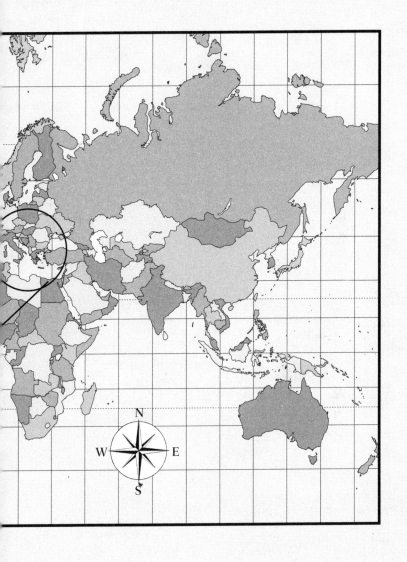

GLOBAL PROTECTION FORCE FILE ON
JACK STALWART

Jack Stalwart applied to be a secret
agent for the Global Protection
Force four months ago.

My name is Jack Stalwart. My older brother,

Max, was a secret agent for you, until he

disappeared on one of your missions. Now I

want to be a secret agent too. If you choose

me, I will be an excellent secret agent and get

rid of evil villains, just like my brother did.

Sincerely,

Jack Stalwart

HIGHLY CONFIDENTIAL

Jack Stalwart was sworn in as a Global Protection Force secret agent four months ago. Since that time, he has completed all of his missions successfully and has stopped no less than twelve evil villains. Because of this he has been assigned the code name "COURAGE."

Jack has yet to uncover the whereabouts of his brother, Max, who is still working for this organization at a secret location. Do not give Secret Agent Jack Stalwart this information. He is never to know about his brother.

Gerald Barter

Gerald Barter
Director, Global Protection Force

THINGS YOU'LL FIND IN EVERY BOOK

Watch Phone: The only gadget Jack wears all the time, even when he's not on official business. His Watch Phone is the central gadget that makes most others work. There are lots of important features, most importantly the "C" button, which reveals the code of the day—necessary to unlock Jack's Secret Agent Book Bag. There are buttons on both sides, one of which ejects his life-saving Melting Ink Pen. Beyond these functions, it also works as a phone and, of course, gives Jack the time of day.

Global Protection Force (GPF): The GPF is the organization Jack works for. It's a worldwide force of young secret agents whose aim is to protect the world's people, places and possessions. No one knows exactly where its main offices are located (all correspondence and gadgets for repair are sent to a special PO Box, and training is held at various locations around the world), but Jack thinks it's somewhere cold, like the Arctic Circle.

Whizzy: Jack's magical miniature globe. Almost every night at precisely 7:30 P.M., the GPF uses Whizzy to send Jack the identity of the country that he must travel to. Whizzy can't talk, but he can cough up messages. Jack's parents don't know Whizzy is anything more than a normal globe.

The Magic Map: The magical map hanging on Jack's bedroom wall. Unlike most maps, the GPF's map is made of a mysterious wood. Once Jack inserts the country piece from Whizzy, the map swallows Jack whole and sends him away on his missions. When he returns, he arrives precisely one minute after he left.

Secret Agent Book Bag: The Book Bag that Jack wears on every adventure. Licensed only to GPF secret agents, it contains top-secret gadgets necessary to foil bad guys and escape certain death. To activate the bag before each mission, Jack must punch in a secret code given to him by his Watch Phone. Once he's away, all he has to do is place his finger on the zip, which identifies him as the owner of the bag and immediately opens.

THE STALWART FAMILY

Jack's dad, John

He moved the family to England when Jack was two, in order to take a job with an aerospace company. As far as Jack knows, his dad designs and manufactures airplane parts. Jack's dad thinks he is an ordinary boy and that his other son, Max, attends a school in Switzerland. Jack's dad is American and his mum is British, which makes Jack a bit of both.

Jack's mum, Corinne

One of the greatest mums as far as Jack is concerned. When she and her husband received a letter from a posh school in Switzerland inviting Max to attend, they were overjoyed. Since Max left six months ago, they have received numerous notes in Max's handwriting telling them he's OK. Little do they know it's all a lie and that it's the GPF sending those letters.

Jack's older brother, Max

Two years ago, at the age of nine, Max joined the GPF. Max used to tell Jack about his adventures and show him how to work his secret-agent gadgets. When the family received a letter inviting Max to attend a school in Europe, Jack figured it was to do with the GPF. Max told him he was right, but that he couldn't tell Jack anything about why he was going away.

Nine-year-old Jack Stalwart

Four months ago, Jack received an anonymous note saying: "Your brother is in danger. Only you can save him." As soon as he could, Jack applied to be a secret agent too. Since that time, he's battled some of the world's most dangerous villains, and hopes some day in his travels to find and rescue his brother, Max.

DESTINATION: *Italy*

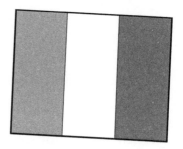

Italy is called *"il Belpaese,"* or "Beautiful Country."

Rome is its capital city.

Today, over 58 million people live in Italy.

The country is divided into twenty regions, including Tuscany and Sardinia.

The Leaning Tower of Pisa is located in the north of the country. It was built over 800 years ago.

The Vatican City, the Pope's "home," is located in Rome.

The Italian national soccer team has won the World Cup four times (1934, 1938, 1982 and 2006) in Rome.

The Great Travel Guide

MOTOR RACING: FACTS AND FIGURES

The world's first racing car was called a De Dion.

Built in 1884 by the French, the De Dion had four wheels, no steering wheel and was powered by steam. It could reach a top speed of 35 miles per hour.

During the 1890s, cars with petrol engines were introduced.

The first proper race between petrol-powered cars and steam-powered engines was called the Paris-Rouen. The petrol-powered car won.

After 1903, races were held at race tracks or "circuits" instead of on roads. The world's first official motor-racing circuit was Brooklands in England.

The "Grand Prix" race was started in 1905 by the French.

There are now many Grand Prix races, in places like Malaysia, Australia, Canada and Germany.

HISTORY OF MONZA

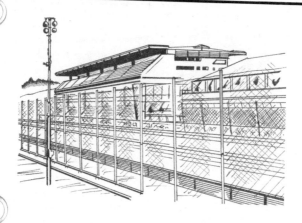

Monza, or Autodromo Nazionale Monza,
is the third oldest motor-racing track in the
world. It was built in 1922.

The track is named Monza after the town
where it's located. Monza is in northern Italy.

Monza is one of the fastest circuits in the
Grand Prix. Drivers can reach speeds of up to
225 miles per hour.

The Italians call Monza "*La Pista Magica*"
or "The Magic Track."

SECRET AGENT GADGET INSTRUCTION MANUAL

Camera Shades: When you need to take photos of someone or something, use the GPF's Camera Shades. Camera Shades look like ordinary sunglasses but are actually a hi-tech digital camera. Just touch the sensor on the top right of the frame to take a picture. Photos can be wired directly to your Watch Phone or can be downloaded from a memory chip hidden inside the frame.

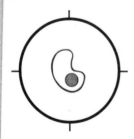

Big Ears: When you need to listen in on a secret conversation, place one of these transparent sticky balls on a person's body. Its hi-tech amplifier will pick up even the slightest sound and send whatever is said into a separate recording device. Perfect when you need to capture a crook admitting to something terrible.

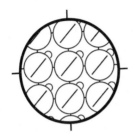

Anti-G Tablets:

The GPF's Anti-G tablets help keep secret agents' bodies working normally when they're traveling at high speeds. Just swallow one of these gray tablets to stop you from passing out. The effect of one tablet lasts up to two hours.

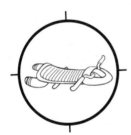

Torpedo: With the push of a button, this lunch-box-sized container transforms into a torpedo-shaped rocket capable of traveling more than 200 miles per hour. Just hop on the seat, grab onto the handles and wait for its hydrogen jets to fire up. Make sure you're wearing your protective gear (goggles and helmet) before setting off. If you're traveling at speeds greater than 100mph, you'll need to take an Anti-G tablet (see above).

Chapter 1:
The Championship

CRASH!

Jack felt his body jolt backward and then forward. He'd been hit from behind.

"I'm going to get you for that!" he yelled to his friend Richard. Richard had just slammed into Jack with his go-kart, sending him into an inflatable barrier.

"Not if you can't catch me!" Richard yelled as he leaned forward onto his steering wheel and cruised past Jack.

1

Jack and Richard were in their friend Charlie Abbott's back garden celebrating his tenth birthday. Because it was a Saturday, Charlie's parents had hired three go-karts for an hour of fun-filled racing. Richard, Jack and Charlie were competing against each other to see who would win the Abbott Family Go-Kart Grand Prix.

Jack put his foot on the accelerator, but the front end of his go-kart was stuck. The marshal jumped over and pushed Jack's go-kart back on course. Turning his wheel gently to the right, he aimed for the corner ahead.

BANG!

Jack side-swiped Charlie, who was trying to get by on the inside.

"Sorry!" Jack smiled slyly as he sped away in hot pursuit of Richard.

"You dog!" yelled Charlie, trying to catch up.

As Jack rounded the corner, he could see
Richard ahead. Richard was looking over
his shoulder at Jack, and he didn't see
another barrier in front of his kart.

BOING!

Richard's kart bounced into the soft
barrier. In the time it took for the marshal
to help Richard out, Jack had come up
alongside him. Now the two boys were
neck-and-neck.

Jack put his foot down and willed his go-kart to cross the line first. When it did, it was by a hair. Jack was the winner of the Abbott Family Grand Prix! The entire party cheered and whistled.

At the "official" award ceremony, Jack, Charlie and Richard stood on the podium that Charlie's dad had made and accepted their medals.

"Lucky break," said Richard, looking up at Jack from the block just below.

As Jack accepted his gold medal, he looked down at the foil-wrapped medallion. He knew there was a delicious disc of milk chocolate inside.

Climbing down, the boys found a spot on the grass and opened their treats. As Jack sat there with Richard and Charlie, he thought about how much fun he was having and how much he liked hanging out with his friends.

"Time to get going," said a voice from across the garden. Jack looked up. It was his dad walking toward him.

Jack licked the chocolate off his fingers. "OK," he said as he stood up and turned to his friends. "See you at school on Monday, guys."

"See ya," said Richard.

"Later," said Charlie, lifting his hand.

"Happy birthday!" said Jack. He slapped his hand into Charlie's before walking over to join his dad.

Jack and his father thanked Mr. and Mrs. Abbott for the fun afternoon. Climbing into the backseat, Jack was still glowing with delight as his dad started the engine and the two of them drove away.

Chapter 2:
The Fanatic

As soon as Jack got home, he walked through the kitchen and past the table where his mum left the mail.

Excellent! thought Jack when he spied a parcel in the shape of a magazine that was addressed to him. It was *Fast Cars*, the number one magazine for fans of the Grand Prix racing competition, and one of Jack's favorites.

Ever since Jack was young, he'd had a thing for cars. As soon as he could walk, he'd toddle over to the front window and watch them speed down the road. At one-and-a-half years old, he was asking his parents to read his dad's car magazines to him. Not surprisingly, one of Jack's first words was "Maserati."

His brother, Max, loved cars too and they used to argue over which car was the most beautiful. As Jack and Max grew older, they became interested in other things like football and swimming, but they never lost their passion for cars.

Secretly, Jack longed to become a racing-car driver, just like his hero, Morgan Parks. Morgan Parks was one of the youngest racing-car drivers on the Grand Prix circuit. From the time Morgan was nine, he was winning local go-kart races, and by fifteen had won the World Go-Kart Champion-ships. Now that he was twenty, he was old enough to drive in a Grand Prix. And not for just any racing team, but for the Italians.

Morgan had become so good that he was close to winning his first World Championship. All he had to do was beat the previous year's winner, Kurt Weber, in the upcoming Grand Prix at Monza, in Italy. The world was holding its breath to see if he could do it.

In fact, Morgan was on the cover of this month's *Fast Cars* magazine. Inside was a story telling the readers what they needed to know about him and the Monza Grand Prix. By now all Jack could think about doing was getting upstairs, finding somewhere comfy to sit and reading all of the juicy details.

Chapter 3:
The Destination

As Jack carried his magazine upstairs, he glanced at Max's room on the way and wondered if his brother, wherever he was, was thinking about the race too.

Jack closed his bedroom door behind him, lay on his bed and got comfortable. Opening his magazine to page eighty-two, he began to read through the life story of his racing hero.

Just as he was getting to the bit about the weekend's race, a familiar sound came from over his left shoulder. He

looked over to his bedside table, and
there was his magical globe, Whizzy,
spinning wildly. It was 7:30 P.M.

"Ahem!" Whizzy coughed and spat out
a jigsaw piece.

Jack quickly closed his magazine,
leaving it on the bed, and leaped onto
the floor. He picked up the piece, which
was in the shape of a boot.

Most countries, as far as Jack could tell,
didn't have a special shape. But this
country did. There was only one country in
the world that looked like a boot, and
that was Italy.

Bellissimo! thought Jack, who had been
to Italy before and loved it. His parents
had taken him and Max there once when
they were younger.

Walking over to his Magic Map, Jack put
the piece where it belonged. Almost
instantly, the name "ITALY" appeared and

then vanished. Jack quickly went back to
his bed and pulled out his Book Bag.

He tapped his Watch Phone and asked it for the code of the day. When the GPF sent back the word T-O-M-A-T-O, Jack nearly laughed out loud. He opened the bag, making sure that he had all his gadgets. Inside were his Camera Shades, Voice-Capture Device and the Torpedo. As he closed his bag and threw it over his shoulder, he stepped toward the Magic Map. The purple light inside Italy was glowing now.

When the time was right, Jack yelled, "Off to Italy!" Then the light flickered and burst, swallowing him into the Magic Map.

Chapter 4:
The Surprise

When Jack arrived, it was daytime and he
was seated in a massive grandstand.
Down below was an enormous racing
track. All around him were men, women
and children, mostly dressed in red.
Across the way, some spectators held up
a red flag. Jack's eyes widened. It was
the flag of the Italian racing team. As Jack
sat there, the crowd started to chant.

  "La Pista Magica!"

  "La Pista Magica!"

From the stories in *Fast Cars* magazine,
Jack knew that *La Pista Magica* meant
"The Magic Track."

As he was trying to figure out whether
he was on a mission or in the middle of a
dream, a loud noise ripped through the
air from below.

VAROOOM!

17

Quickly, Jack looked to see a Grand Prix racing car speed by in front of the stand.

He blinked a few times. Is this for real? he thought.

VAROOOM!

A red flash of color flew by. The crowd went wild. They stood up and began to cheer.

"Morgan!"

"Morgan!"

It was his hero.

VAROOOM!

Another speeding car raced by. This time it was silver. It was the German driver.

Jack sat there, stunned. There was no way he was this lucky. But looking around at the stands, the people and the cars, there was no way he was anywhere else. Jack was the luckiest boy alive. He was sitting in the grandstand at one of the most famous racing tracks in the world. Jack was at Monza watching the practice lap before tomorrow's Grand Prix.

Chapter 5:
The Introduction

Just then, Jack felt something tickle his ear. He thought he could hear somebody whispering to him from behind.

Carefully, he looked over his shoulder. Sitting behind him was a man wearing a navy-blue suit and expensive sunglasses. Behind the shaded lenses, Jack could see the man's eyes nervously darting all over the place.

"Come with me," he said softly as he placed his hand on Jack's shoulder.

Jack pulled away. He didn't like it when strangers touched him.

"Come with me," the man said again. From his accent, Jack could tell that he was Italian.

"Why should I?" said Jack, who decided it was a good idea to be cautious.

"Because I'm the one who called the GPF," said the man. Before Jack could respond, he carried on. "Sorry to seem so serious," he said, leaning a bit closer. "But I need to be careful. My name is Roberto Panini." Putting his hand out to Jack, he added, "I'm the boss of the Italian team."

Jack gulped as he shook Mr. Panini's hand. He couldn't believe he'd been called in by the head of one of the most famous motor-racing teams in history. Jack didn't recognize him with his sunglasses on.

"What can I do for you?" he asked as
he looked at the man. Roberto was about
fifty-five, with mostly black hair, except for
some silver streaks.

"Not here," said Roberto. "There are too
many people," he added, looking around.
"We need to find a place to talk."

Jack looked around too. Although most of the fans were focused on the track, you could never be sure who was listening in on conversations, especially in crowds.

"Come with me," Roberto said, standing and motioning for Jack to follow him out of the viewing area.

VAROOM!

Another racing car screeched by. This time, Jack recognized it as one of the French team's cars.

Roberto climbed the steps and disappeared from view. Jack followed and found himself at the top of a large walkway that wound itself around the stadium. Roberto and Jack walked the entire length and down another flight of stairs until they were on the ground.

Moving quickly, Jack followed Mr. Panini through the crowds and toward a grassy area to the right. When he got to a lone tree, Roberto stopped and turned to Jack.

He took his sunglasses off. "The reason I have called you here today," he said, getting to the point, "is that I think someone is trying to hurt my star driver." As if Jack didn't know who that was, Roberto added, "Somebody is trying to eliminate Morgan Parks."

Chapter 6:
The Cover

"What?" said Jack, who was completely stunned. He couldn't believe anyone would think of harming another person, let alone his racing idol.

Mr. Panini let out a big sigh. "During a routine check this morning, our chief engineer found a faulty brake pipe in car number one," he explained.

Jack knew that Morgan drove car number one; Manuel Garcia drove car number two. He also knew that the brakes on all cars worked because of pressure put on the brake pads by fluid inside the brake pipes.

If the brake pipe was broken, the fluid would leak out, causing the brakes to fail. In a car driving 200 miles per hour, that would spell disaster for a driver like Morgan Parks.

"How do you know that someone tampered with it?" Jack asked. "Is it possible that it could have cracked on its own?" He pretty much knew the answer to that question, but he had to ask it anyway.

Roberto looked at Jack. "Absolutely not. Plus, the pipe looked like someone had bashed it with something. I can't have Morgan hurt before tomorrow's race," he said. "I need you to figure out who did this and make sure they don't try it again."

"What makes you think they will?"

asked Jack, figuring that once their plan failed the first time they might not want to risk getting caught the second.

"There's too much riding on this race not to," said Roberto.

Jack agreed. Morgan was about to lead the Italians to this year's championship. With Morgan out of the picture, it would make way for another team to grab the title.

"The best way for me to work out who's behind this," offered Jack, "is to go undercover."

Roberto was listening carefully. "What do you suggest?"

"Why don't I pretend that I'm a reporter for *Fast Cars* magazine?" Jack said.

He decided he knew enough about the magazine to pretend that he worked for them. "Let's say I'm doing a story called 'Twenty-four Hours Before the Race,'" he added. "You've granted me unlimited access to the cars, crew and drivers so that I can write about what it's really like behind the scenes."

Jack carried on, "It's a perfect way for me to interview and observe everyone involved without anyone catching on. And if we're lucky, the person who did it might forget I'm there and slip up."

"I like your thinking," said Roberto, nodding his head. He seemed pleased with Jack's ideas.

"But before I begin," said Jack, "I'd like to get an idea of who you think is behind this."

Roberto's eyes scanned the field. "It could be anyone," he said, letting out another big sigh. "It could be a member of my crew, another driver, a sponsor . . . anyone."

"Have you said anything to Morgan?" asked Jack.

"No," said Roberto. "The only person who is aware that something happened is the chief engineer. Speaking about Morgan," he added, "I need him to stay focused. When we discovered the brake pipe had been damaged, we had to give him the number two car. We told our workers it was due to 'technical problems' on Morgan's car."

"Don't worry," said Jack, trying to reassure Mr. Panini. "I'll find out who's responsible. I'm a big fan of Morgan and the team," he added.

"Good," said Mr. Panini, looking a bit more relaxed. "I asked for someone who knew about cars." He smiled at Jack. "Here's my business card with my mobile number on it. We'll need to keep this conversation between us," he added.

Jack reached into his Book Bag and pulled out his Morphing Badge. The Morphing Badge was a plastic badge tied to a thin chain. It had a near-invisible keyboard on the other side that a secret agent could use to program information. Whatever he or she typed would appear on the front, next to the picture of the secret agent that was already there.

Jack quickly typed in:

PRESS PASS

FAST CARS MAGAZINE

Name: Jack Stuart

When the badge was finished, Jack put the chain around his neck. "Ready," he said.

"Fantastic," said Roberto, putting his sunglasses back on. "Now, let me take you to the crew."

Chapter 7:
The Star

They left the tree and followed a path up some steps, across a bridge and over the circuit until they reached the ground on the other side.

When Jack entered the "pit garage"— the room where the team, drivers and the cars were—he noticed that Morgan had just pulled in after finishing his qualifying lap. He had the second fastest time of the day, which meant that later on he'd get a chance to race for pole position. Pole position meant the first car to start in the next day's race.

"Great lap, Morgan!" said one of the team members, tapping Morgan on the helmet as he climbed out of the car. He was dressed head-to-toe in the Italian team's famous red racing suit.

Jack stood and watched as Morgan took off his helmet. Underneath was a fire-proof material that covered his wavy brown hair. Then he took off the Head and Neck Support plate, or HANS, which sat behind his neck to protect it in case of an accident.

He tried not to be, but Jack was star-

struck. Here he was in the same room as one of the greatest drivers of all time.

"Fantastic job, Morgan," Roberto said to his driver, giving him the thumbs-up. "Let's see if we can get pole." Then Roberto quickly changed the subject to address the crew. "This is Jack Stuart, everyone. He's a junior reporter for one of my favorite magazines, *Fast Cars*."

Everyone in the box went quiet and looked at Jack.

Roberto carried on, "As a favor to my friend, the editor, I've agreed to let him be a bit of a 'fly on the wall' over the next twenty-four hours. He'll have unlimited access to all of you and the cars. Just go about your business and pretend he's not here," he said. "But when you see him, make sure you treat him well."

With that, Roberto patted Jack on the back and left him standing at the front of the room. He had a feeling the crew was wondering what to do with a nine-year-old kid.

"Hey there!" said a voice from the side. Jack was too deep in thought to realize it was Morgan Parks making his way over.

"So," he said, looking at Jack's badge, "you work for *Fast Cars*?"

Jack stammered a bit and then gathered himself. He looked up at the twenty-year-old. "Sure do," he said as he put out his hand. "It's great to meet you. I'm a really big fan."

Morgan laughed and shook Jack's hand. "That's what they all say. That is, until I lose. And then somebody else will have my fans."

Jack couldn't help but like Morgan. He seemed like a great guy. "Do you think I could interview you later?" Jack asked. He thought it might be a good idea to look for any information that might lead to a possible suspect.

"Sure," said Morgan. "How about after the next qualifying round? I'll have a few minutes then."

"Great," said Jack, feeling pretty excited.

"You know," Morgan said, looking at Jack, "I was about your age when I started karting." It looked as though he was thinking about some happy memories. "Well," he said, remembering where he was, "I'd better get going."

Morgan walked off, leaving Jack at the front of the room. The crew was busy swarming over his car, checking the engine's on-board computer and the driver's statistics from the qualifying lap.

Now, Jack figured, was the perfect time
to watch the people who had the most
contact with the car and the biggest
opportunity to hurt Morgan Parks.

Chapter 8:
The Pit Garage

From what Jack could tell there were two kinds of people there—the engineers and the mechanics. The engineers were responsible for designing the car and watching its progress during the race. The mechanics were there to fix any problems and keep the car in good working order. From what Jack could tell there were eight of each, making sixteen people (and sixteen suspects) in the garage with access to Morgan's car.

Jack watched each of them carefully as they worked on the car. From what he could see, there wasn't anything strange about what they were doing.

Just then, Jack heard some high-pitched clicking over his right shoulder. He quickly turned to see a row of photographers taking pictures from outside.

"Morgan!" one of them yelled, trying to get his attention. When Morgan turned to pose for the man, dozens of flashing lights went off.

"Thanks!" yelled another as the crew of photographers moved on to the Japanese pit garage, which was next door.

When the photographers had cleared, Morgan turned to chat to the chief engineer, who had a special badge on his suit.

As the two men were speaking, the famous movie star Hugh Perry and his friends strolled in. Jack knew who it was because he was known for collecting expensive cars. He brushed by Jack, not taking any notice of him, and made his way over to Morgan. Morgan greeted Hugh by shaking his hand and giving him a hug.

After a few quick words where the actor wished Morgan "Good luck, man," he and his crowd turned and left.

Then, as if Morgan hadn't had enough visitors, Jack heard another voice that sounded familiar. It had a German accent. Jack turned to see who it was. It was Kurt Weber, the lead driver for the French. He was wearing his team's signature light-blue racing suit.

Jack knew it was common for the driver and the maker of his car to be from different countries. Kurt was a German

driving a French car; Morgan was British
driving for an Italian team.

"My friend!" Kurt said, walking over to
Morgan with his arms outstretched.
Morgan's reaction, although polite, told
Jack that Kurt wasn't one of his mates.

"What's up, Kurt?" asked Morgan, keeping it short.

"So sorry to see you in second place," said the German, who spoke as though his jaws were wired shut. "I guess I'm running a bit quicker than you today."

"Yeah," said Morgan, faking a smile. "I guess."

"Well," said Kurt, "see you over my shoulder in the next round." He spun on his heels and left the garage.

"That guy is so annoying," said Morgan, turning to the chief engineer. "The reason I came second was because he squeezed me out at the last corner."

"Sparky!" yelled another voice passing by the garage. Jack knew that "Sparky" was one of Morgan's nicknames.

Morgan looked at the door, but this time a smile spread across his face. Jack recognized the driver walking in. It was

Carlos Gomez, the Spanish driver for the German team. Jack had read that Morgan and Carlos were friends.

After a quick chat, Carlos left Morgan, who began to put on his helmet for the next qualifying round.

When he and the car were ready, Morgan climbed in. The team pushed the car out of the garage and onto the side road. He started the car and revved its ten-cylinder engine.

VAROOM!

Once the crew had completed the final checks, Morgan tore off down the track and waited for the last of the qualifying laps to start. Driving in just under 1 minute and 21 seconds, Morgan set a new track record and, to everyone's delight—other than Kurt Weber's—snatched the next day's pole position out of the French team's hands.

Chapter 9:
The Press Conference

Afterward, Jack heard some of the crew talking about a "press conference." He followed Morgan and the crew from the pit garage, over the track and into a tall building made of glass. This was the Monza Media Center, and it was where reporters and photographers got a chance to ask the drivers questions before the next day's big race.

Because Morgan had driven the fastest time of the day, he got to sit in the middle of the table at the front of the room. On either side of him were some of the other drivers.

As Jack took his place at the back, he stood there thinking about his secret identity. It was perfect. Being a reporter gave him the chance to observe an entire room of suspects—from the drivers to the owners, they were all there. And because

he was such a fan, he recognized nearly everyone.

Seated at the driver's table were: Jake, from the American team; Carlos, from the German team; Morgan, from the Italian team; Kurt, from the French team; and Marcus, from the Japanese team.

Since anyone in the room could be a suspect, Jack grabbed his Voice-Capture Device, or VCD. This small yellow box could record a speaker's voice and tell you if he or she were a criminal. Knowing that most crooks didn't stop at one crime, Jack figured that if there was a bad guy in the room, there was a chance that he or she could be involved in tampering with Morgan's car.

As he lifted the small yellow box, a voice boomed across the room. "This press conference is about to start!" The crowd quieted down. The first reporter asked his question.

"So," he said, "Morgan, can you tell us why you're using Manuel's car in tomorrow's race? After all, we know it's your team's number two."

"Well," said Morgan, leaning into the microphone, "my usual car has 'technical

difficulties' and the engineers and
mechanics are looking into the problem."

"How confident do you feel about

winning?" said another, directing his question to Morgan.

"Pretty confident," Morgan replied, smiling.

Jack took a look at the VCD. There was no flashing light going off, which meant Morgan was as honest as Jack thought.

"What about you, Kurt?" said a female reporter, who said she worked for the *Monza News*.

"Well, you know," he answered, "I have felt confident all along that we will defend our title. Whatever it takes," he added, grinning at the audience.

Jack glanced at the gadget again. The small red light on the top was flashing now. He punched a few buttons and downloaded the information. There was a screen to the right of the light. It read:

```
KURT WEBER

^

ARRESTED AT 16 YEARS OF AGE

FOR STEALING AND JOYRIDING

IN CARS

^

ARREST DETAILS KEPT FROM

PUBLIC DUE TO JUVENILE STATUS
```

Although Kurt had been in trouble a long
time ago, Jack thought it was interesting
that the crime involved tampering with
and stealing a car.

"Marcus," said a female reporter from
Race magazine, "you're fourth in the
standings. How will that affect your driving
tomorrow?"

"Like I have nothing to lose," he replied.

Jack thought his comment was interesting. He looked down at the VCD. It was

flashing red again. When Jack downloaded the information, he was surprised to see the result.

MARCUS CHARLES

^

ARRESTED AT 15 YEARS OF AGE
FOR STEALING AND JOYRIDING
IN CARS

^

ARREST DETAILS KEPT FROM
PUBLIC DUE TO JUVENILE STATUS

Jack's eyes widened. As crazy as it seemed, he began to wonder whether Kurt or Marcus or both could be involved in damaging Morgan's car. After all, they had similar arrest records and they obviously knew their way around cars. The team bosses who hired them wouldn't have known about their past histories because their records had been sealed.

"Mr. Slater," said an unknown reporter to a member of the audience, "what will it do to your sponsorship of the French team if they don't win the title this year?"

The spotlight flashed onto a man sitting in the second row. He was wearing a cream-colored suit. There was nothing unusual about him except for his nose, which was crooked, and the flashy watch on his left wrist, which Jack knew cost a lot of money.

Jack recognized him as the president of Fizzy Pop, one of the world's most popular soft-drink brands. Fizzy Pop was sold everywhere from London to Thailand—they were huge.

Because Fizzy Pop sponsored the French team, Jack thought it was a fair question. After all, the sponsors were the ones who had the most to lose. They gave millions to the racing teams to win these championships, and in return the teams became moving advertisements for their brands. Jack was interested in what he had to say too.

Mr. Slater cleared his throat. "We are proud sponsors whatever happens tomorrow."

Jack looked at his VCD. Nothing showed up. Mr. Slater was "clean."

After Mr. Slater had finished speaking, someone called across to the drivers that the press conference was over. They stood up and began to walk out, one by one. Jack might not be a real reporter, but he thought the press conference was very helpful. After all, he'd gathered some interesting information.

Chapter 10:
The Interview

After the press conference, Jack caught up with Morgan back at the pit garage. He was alone, checking up on his gear.

"Hi, Morgan," said Jack, trying not to surprise him from behind.

"Hiya, kid," he said, spinning around.

"Is it all right if I interview you now?" asked Jack.

"Sure," said Morgan. "I'm pretty much finished with my set-up for tomorrow." He perched himself on a tall chair next to where he was standing.

"So, tell me," Jack started, "how do you rate your chances for tomorrow?" He felt a bit silly asking the same question as the other reporters, but he needed Morgan to think he was for real.

"Pretty good, I think," he said. "As long as Kurt plays fair, I'll have a clear shot at the title."

Jack agreed with that statement. "On that note," he asked, "can you tell me a bit about Kurt and Marcus Charles, the driver for Japan?" He thought it might be interesting to find out more about those two from someone who knew them.

"Just that they came through the ranks like I did," Morgan explained. "Except they were ten years earlier. Kurt was the fastest go-kart racer in the world," he explained, "until I finally broke his record at the Go-Kart Championship."

"Kurt must have been pretty annoyed," said Jack, who couldn't help but notice a similarity with this year's Grand Prix. Morgan was about to knock Kurt from his first-place perch again. That would give Kurt a possible motive.

"Yeah," he said. "I'm sure he was. But you can't stay on top forever. You have to expect that sooner or later you're going to be replaced. He had his fifteen minutes of fame. And now," he added, "I guess I have mine."

Morgan looked at his watch. "Well," he said, looking at Jack, "I have to get some sleep."

"Of course," said Jack, who knew racing-car drivers needed as much sleep as possible. Morgan waved goodbye to Jack and closed the door behind him.

Jack sat there, alone in the pit garage. He glanced over at Morgan's car. Figuring this was a good time to check it out, he began to walk toward it. But as he did so, he heard some loud whispering on the other side of the door. In case it had something to do with the case, he decided to hide and listen for clues.

Quickly, Jack grabbed his Klimbing Kit out of his Book Bag. On the side of its circular case was a hatch that released a powerful nylon rope for climbing. Jack opened the hatch and pointed the opening toward the rafters on the ceiling. As soon as he pushed the "eject" button, the rope shot out and twirled around one of the steel beams.

Jack had to hurry. The voices were getting louder and someone was turning the doorknob.

He tugged on the rope to make sure it was secure. Using the strength in his arms, he pulled himself upward, scrambling toward the beams. As soon as he reached the top, he yanked the cord back into its case, just as two people entered the room.

Chapter 11:
The Fall

When Jack looked down, he saw Kurt
Weber and Marcus Charles. Quickly, he
flicked on the recording feature on his
VCD. He wanted to capture them speaking
in case they admitted to something.

"Now, let's fix this for good," snickered
Kurt. "I'm sick of this guy always getting
in our way."

"Yeah," said Marcus. "I don't know how
they found the crack in the pipe. But
there's no way they're going to see this
one coming."

As Marcus was speaking, Jack spied Kurt plugging a wire into a socket behind the driver's seat. This was where the engine management computer was kept.

"A few more instructions," said Kurt, punching some commands into a handheld device at the other end of the wire, "and the throttle will stay open until . . . *KABOOM!*" Kurt opened his fingers in the air, as if he were showing Marcus the way a bomb exploded.

Jack gulped. The throttle was what controlled the speed of the engine. If it stayed open, then the engine would go faster and faster until it eventually exploded. Normally, the driver and the engine management system would step in. But Kurt was doing something that meant nothing and no one would be able to shut it down.

"That should do it," said Marcus to Kurt as Kurt removed the plug from the car. The two of them stood there grinning from ear to ear. Jack, on the other hand, was totally horrified. Although he had suspected them, he couldn't believe they could sink this low.

He had to stop Kurt and Marcus. Keeping his gaze on the two men, he reached for a gadget in his Book Bag. But as he did so, he lost his footing. Jack's legs slipped out from underneath him and he fell sideways

off the beam. Instinctively, he grabbed
onto the steel bar with both hands but, in
doing so, let go of his VCD. The gadget fell
to the floor and smashed into hundreds of
little pieces. With all the noise, the two
men looked up.

"Well, well," said Kurt, spying Jack's legs dangling just above him. "What do we have here? A little snitch," he went on, kicking the broken bits of the VCD everywhere.

The weight of Jack's body was causing him to lose his grip. He tried desperately to pull himself back up, but he couldn't.

"We can't let this kid tell anyone what we've done," said Marcus. "It'll ruin your chances for tomorrow, not to mention our careers and the money."

Jack played over in his mind what Marcus had said . . . your chances for tomorrow . . . the money. Not only were they doing this so Kurt could win, but also because someone was paying them to do it. That meant there were more than two people involved in this crime.

"Looks like we'll have to take care of this little problem," said Marcus.

Kurt jumped up and grabbed onto Jack's right foot. He pulled hard, causing Jack to tumble directly into Marcus's arms. Marcus pinned Jack's wrists behind his back and held them there.

"Let go of me!" shouted Jack as he tried to wriggle free.

"Oh no, you don't," said Kurt. "We're not going to let a little pipsqueak like you ruin our chances. We're going to put you somewhere where no one will find you. At least not until after tomorrow when I reclaim the title, and then no one will believe you." He gave an evil smile.

"You're not going to get away with this!" Jack shouted.

By now, Kurt had pulled some tape out of one of the mechanics' tool drawers and ripped off a piece. He covered Jack's mouth with it to stop him from speaking. Jack tried to scream through the tape, but

trying to make a loud noise when your lips
are sealed is totally impossible.

Kurt returned to the drawers. He was looking for something else. Pulling out a long, thin copper wire, he walked back over to Jack.

"If there had been rope, I would have used it," he said. "But this is all they've got." He lifted it in front of Jack's eyes. "Sorry, this is going to hurt." He walked around behind Jack and pulled out a length of wire.

When Jack took the GPF's self-defense class, they taught him that if an attacker has you by the wrists then the best way to break free is to stamp on the top of the attacker's foot bone. Jack lifted his strongest leg and pounded down onto Marcus's foot.

"Owwww!" Marcus yelped as he let go of Jack to grab his sore foot.

Before Kurt could catch him, Jack made a break for it. He slid onto the floor and

toward the back door. But as he pulled
himself up to reach for the handle,
something crashed onto the top of his
head. It hit him so violently that the pain
made him drop to his knees.

He wasn't sure whether it was Kurt or Marcus who had come from behind. In his dazed state, he could feel his wrists being tied behind his back with that copper wire. It hurt a lot, but he didn't care. He was so dizzy that he slumped to the floor and completely passed out.

Chapter 12:
The Locker

When Jack woke up, he found himself
sitting with his knees pulled up to his
chest in what seemed like a very small
space. Thankfully he still had his Book
Bag. Kurt and Marcus probably hadn't
thought to take it. But Jack had lost all his
evidence when the VCD went crashing to
the floor.

Although it was dark, he could feel that
there were walls on all sides of his body.
When he tried to push his legs outward,
he couldn't. Given how big he was, he

guessed the space was almost three feet wide and about the same height. He wriggled onto his knees and tried to stand up. It felt as though he were in some sort of closet.

Instead of sitting there in darkness, Jack figured the best next step was to turn on his Everglo Light. The only problem was that his wrists were tied behind his back.

Luckily for Jack, when Kurt and Marcus had tied them together, they'd done it high enough so that he could still move his hands up, down and sideways.

Stretching one of his fingers over to his Watch Phone, he activated his Everglo Light. A bright glow lit up the space. It looked like he wasn't in a closet after all, but in some sort of steel locker.

Excellent, Jack thought. Although he'd just been attacked by two criminals, it was still a good day. They might have tied his wrists together, but he could reach his Melting Ink Pen. It was the only gadget that could eat through steel and it was just within reach at the side of his Watch Phone.

He used one finger to eject it, and another two to grab hold. Then, with his fingers, he twisted the top of the pen. Rubbing the pen back and forth over the copper wire, he waited for it to do its magic. When he heard a small snap, he knew he'd broken free.

As he brought his wrists around, he realized they were sore. The wire had cut into his skin and it was almost bleeding. Reaching into his Book Bag, Jack grabbed his Fix-It Tape. He peeled off two strips and wrapped one around each wrist.

The special formula in the tape instantly made his skin feel better.

Now that his hands were free, he had some work to do. He had to get himself out of this locker. Not only was he running out of fresh air, he was also worried about Morgan Parks. If Jack had been in there as long as he thought, there was a chance he'd missed the race. And if what Kurt had done to Morgan's car worked, then the Italian team and their star driver were history.

He stood up and drew a circle on the door with his Melting Ink Pen. Just then, he heard voices outside. *Yikes!* Jack thought as he watched the chemicals begin to eat through the steel locker door. The last thing he needed was for Marcus and Kurt to find him trying to escape. As the hole in the locker sizzled

away, Jack could hear what the voices said.

"How's your guy doing?" said the first voice. It was an American man. Although Jack was relieved, he couldn't very well ask for help. For all he knew, one or both of these guys could be involved in the plot to hurt Morgan.

"Great," said the second. "It's the thirty-fifth lap and Jake's in fifth place. We swapped wings to help the downforce. It seems to be working."

Thank goodness, Jack thought. From what he could tell, the race was still going on. Since the man didn't mention it, he figured Morgan's car hadn't exploded yet. Jack still had some time.

"We've done the same on Carlos's car," said the second voice. "The track is running pretty fast." Jack guessed it was a member of the German team. "Carlos is having the race of his career," the man added. "Fourth position, and only three seconds behind Marcus."

Jack heard what sounded like running taps. Then he heard a hand drier before a door closed and everything was silent. The two men must have left the room. When the chemical from the pen had eaten through the steel, Jack punched through it and a circle of metal popped out onto the floor.

Crawling out of the locker, he noticed that he was in some sort of men's changing room. He hoped it wasn't too far from the Italians' pit garage. Jack had to get to them to stop the race—Morgan Parks' life depended on it.

Chapter 13:
The Problem

Jack rushed through the changing room and made his way outside. From what he could tell, he was at the other end of the circuit, far away from the Italian team.

VAROOM!

The cars were whizzing around furiously. Across the track and over in the grand-stands, the crowd was going wild. Jack looked quickly at the scoreboard and noticed that Morgan was in first place. He was now on lap forty, which meant he had only thirteen to go.

It looked like Morgan wasn't returning to the pits again. He'd already made his two stops. Jack knew the Italians had a plan of stopping no more than twice to change tires and refuel. Jack's only hope was to call Mr. Panini so that he could radio Morgan in the car and warn him. But when he dialed Mr. Panini's number there was no answer.

Drat, thought Jack. Morgan was out there all alone.

He had to do something. But catching a racing car at Monza is a tricky thing. Unless you have the Torpedo, that is, in which case it's not only easy, it's fun.

Chapter 14:
The Rocket

Jack unzipped his Book Bag and pulled out a torpedo-shaped canister about the size of a lunch-box. He placed it on the ground and pushed a few buttons on his Watch Phone. The Torpedo opened from the middle and a seat big enough for two people to sit on popped out.

He then pushed another button and the nose of the canister grew, as did the tail. At the same time two handles came out of the front and hydrogen powered jets burst from the back.

Reaching into his Book Bag, Jack pulled out his Anti-G tablets.

The GPF's Anti-G tablets helped to protect an agent's body when they were riding on something super fast. After popping a few in his mouth, Jack put on a transparent, soft hat that hardened almost immediately. He then placed his Anti-Detection Visor over his eyes to protect them from flying debris.

Normally, the Anti-Detection Visor would be transparent, but whenever secret agents needed to hide their identity, they could change the shade from transparent to silver. That way no one could see their faces.

Jack did just that, since he knew there were lots of TV cameras around. He turned on the ignition and sped off into the air.

Whizzing over trees and the barrier that

ran alongside the track, Jack nose-dived
toward the ground and headed straight
for the cars ahead.

ZOOM!

When the crowd noticed him on the track, Jack could hear them cheer. He thought how funny it must be to see someone whizzing around the track on a rocket.

ZOOM!

Jack blasted by Carlos, the driver for Germany. He could hear him shift down a gear as he spied Jack sailing past.

ZOOM!

He swiftly cruised by Marcus. I'll get you,
Jack thought as he kept his focus on the
car at the front.

ZOOM!

Next up was Kurt, whom he ignored,
carrying on until he came alongside
Morgan. When Morgan noticed the
Torpedo, he briefly turned toward Jack.

"Pull over!" Jack yelled, motioning for Morgan to get off the road. "Get out of the car!"

But Morgan didn't respond. There was no way he could tell what Jack was saying. The noise of the engines was far too loud and the silver shade on Jack's visor was too dark for Morgan to realize who it was. Before Jack could deactivate the Anti-Detection Visor, Morgan looked back at the road and sped off again.

"Pull over!" Jack yelled, trying to catch up. "The car's about to explode!"

But Morgan still couldn't hear him. Jack wasn't surprised that he was ignoring him. After all, this was the biggest race of his life. Jack was going to have to think of something else—and fast—or else Morgan Parks and the Italian team were toast.

Just ahead, on the side of a bend, Jack spied a large area with small rocks on the ground. This was a gravel trap—the perfect way to bring Morgan to safety.

ZOOM!

Increasing his speed, Jack finally caught up to Morgan. He waited a moment before nudging the Torpedo Morgan's way. Reacting quickly, Morgan swerved to avoid Jack, skidding to a stop in the middle of the gravel pit.

"What on earth do you think you're doing?" Morgan screamed at Jack, climbing out of his car and shoving open his visor in anger. By now, Jack had pulled up next to the Italian car.

As Jack was about to explain the situation, he heard a horrible noise. It sounded like the engine on Morgan's car was out of control . . . It was about to explode.

"Jump on!" yelled Jack. A puff of oily smoke spat out of the car's exhaust. When Morgan saw this, he knew what was going to happen too. He leaped onto the Torpedo and sat behind Jack.

"Hold on!" shouted Jack as he flicked the handles. The two of them shot off into the distance, just as a massive explosion ripped across the track.

KABOOM!

Chapter 15:
The Flames

As Jack and Morgan sailed away from the explosion and over to the pits, they looked back at the car. One of the world's most beautiful and expensive racing cars was in the middle of a fireball. Flames were spiking toward the sky and Jack could see a fire crew speeding in the direction of the wreck.

When they got to the pit garage, Jack slowed the Torpedo down and let it hover outside. Morgan climbed down, took off his helmet and turned to Jack.

"Who are you?" he said. "You obviously don't work for *Fast Cars*."

"Just a kid who loves cars," said Jack, smiling. Although it was pretty obvious that he was more than a reporter, he decided it was better to keep Morgan in the dark.

"I owe you my life," Morgan said as he placed his hand in Jack's. "Thank you. If you ever need anything—"

At that moment, a group of reporters and photographers appeared in the distance.

"Morgan! Morgan!" they shouted. The young driver turned toward them.

With Morgan's gaze in the other direction, Jack quickly tapped on his Watch Phone, shutting down the Torpedo. He then whipped off his hat and visor and stuffed them and the gadget into his Book Bag.

As the reporters swamped the driver, they forced him away from Jack and over to the far side of the room. Morgan looked at Jack as if to say sorry, and started answering their questions. "What happened out there?" asked one reporter.

"Who was that who saved you?" yelled another reporter.

"Do you think the car will ever race again?" shouted a third.

Just then, Jack heard a noise in the background. It was the crowd. Kurt had crossed the finish line in first place. He'd kept his title as reigning champion of the Grand Prix.

Now that Morgan was safe, Jack had some unfinished business to attend to. There were two drivers and at least one unknown person out there who were responsible for messing with Morgan's car. With an idea of how he could catch all three, Jack hung his press badge back around his neck, walked alongside the other reporters and made his way over to the winner's area.

Chapter 16:
The Winner

The winner's circle was a fifteen-minute walk from the pit garage—the perfect amount of time for Jack to make a few phone calls. By the time he'd arrived, Kurt and Marcus were already there, as was Carlos, who finished in third place for the Germans. Jack blended into the crowd so Kurt and Marcus couldn't see him.

Guessing that whoever hired Kurt and Marcus might try to speak to them at the ceremony, Jack plucked two clear and sticky pea-sized gadgets out of his Book

Bag. These were the GPF's Big Ears, which could pick up very quiet sounds and feed them back into a speaker on an agent's Watch Phone as well as a special recording device in their Book Bag.

Jack tossed one of the Big Ears toward Kurt, where it softly attached itself to the front of his overalls. He threw the other one toward Marcus, and it stuck to the top of his shoulder. Since there was so much commotion going on, neither the drivers nor the crowd noticed what Jack was doing. Finally, he pulled out his Camera Shades and put them on.

As Kurt and Marcus talked to their fans, Jack listened carefully. He heard Kurt showing off to some reporters about how he deserved to win the race. Marcus went on to another about his upbringing in a small town in France. Jack could hear the engineers on either side of the two drivers chatting about next year's race already.

And then, as Jack was standing there, something interesting happened. He saw Kurt's eyes glance and nod to somebody in the crowd. Jack looked in the direction of his gaze and noticed Mr. Slater, the Fizzy Pop president, making his way to the front. Kurt nudged Marcus and they got up to greet him. The reporters started talking to Carlos about coming third.

When Mr. Slater reached the two drivers, the conversation was short, but very interesting. Jack could hear Mr. Slater speak first.

"Well done, boys," he said.

Jack took a few digital photos by pushing a button on his Camera Shades.

"We didn't totally get rid of our competition," said Marcus. "I hope that won't stop us from getting the money," he added.

So, thought Jack, Mr. Slater was the third

criminal. He was the one who hired Kurt and Marcus to damage Morgan's car—and they'd been hoping to hurt him at the same time.

"Not at all," Mr. Slater said. "The most important thing is that the French team won."

At that point, Jack saw Mr. Slater pull two pieces of paper out of his inside jacket pocket. They looked like checks. Jack took some more photos with his Camera Shades. Mr. Slater gave one each to Kurt and Marcus, then escaped back

into the crowd. Jack thought it was time to get the police involved now that he had gathered enough evidence.

At that point, an announcer began to speak.

"Ladies and gentlemen, third place in this year's Monza Grand Prix goes to Carlos Gomez from the German team!" The German team of engineers and mechanics clapped furiously.

"Second place at this year's Monza Grand Prix goes to Marcus Charles of the Japanese team!" The Japanese, who thought they might only come fourth, were delighted with their second-place finish.

"And finally," the announcer said, "the winner of this year's Monza Grand Prix and overall winner of the World Championship is Kurt Weber from the French team!"

At that, the crowd of French supporters

went crazy. Kurt took his place on top of the stand. After they had played the German national anthem for his home country, he shook a huge bottle of champagne, uncorked it and  sprayed it all over his teammates. It was at that point that a police van screeched into the winner's arena. At least ten Italian policemen flung open the back doors and stepped out, fully armed. Jack waved his arms to attract their attention. The police chief charged through the crowd toward him.

"Here's the evidence I was telling you about," said Jack as he handed over the recording from his Big Ears. "This proves that Kurt Weber and Marcus Charles were responsible for damaging Morgan Parks' car. And, most importantly, for trying to hurt him.

"This also proves," he went on, handing over the Camera Shade evidence, "that Mr. Slater, the president of Fizzy Pop, paid them to do it."

Those in the crowd who heard Jack gasped at the news. The police chief's eyes widened with surprise.

"*Grazie*," he said. Then, without missing a beat, he yelled orders to his team in Italian.

Before Kurt and Marcus knew what had happened, six of the policemen pounced on them, pulled their wrists behind their backs and slapped on some handcuffs. The crowd watched in amazement.

As they were dragged through the

crowd, Kurt passed by Jack, who was still standing next to the police chief.

"You little brat!" he hissed. "We'll get you for this!"

"Let's see how you like having your hands tied behind your back," said Jack, pleased that he could get his revenge.

Kurt let out a growl before being shown into the back of the police van. Marcus was led in behind him and then the door was slammed in their faces.

When Mr. Slater noticed the remaining policemen heading for him, he ran in the other direction. They wrestled him to the ground and handcuffed him too before putting him in the van with Marcus and Kurt. The door slammed shut a final time.

The photographers and reporters couldn't believe how lucky they were to capture a story like this. Bulbs were flashing everywhere as they tried to get a photo of the three men.

When the driver of the police van was ready, he flicked on the sirens and red lights.

Not quite the "victory lap" of Monza they're used to, thought Jack. They'd be going away for a long time and would never get the chance to race cars again.

Chapter 17:
The Mentor

"Well done," said a voice from behind Jack. It was Mr. Panini. He looked pleased.

"You did a great job out there," he said. "I can't say I'm happy about the car, but Morgan was what was most important. And you got rid of two of the nastiest drivers on the track," he added, "and caught a sponsor who was as crooked as his nose. A job well done, I'd say."

"I'm glad I was able to help," said Jack, who was also happy.

"You know," said Mr. Panini, "the way

you drove that rocket out there leads me
to believe you'd be a pretty good racing-
car driver yourself."

"Well," said Jack, a bit embarrassed,
"I've always wanted to be one."

"Why don't you tell your parents to give
me a call, and I'll see what I can do to
help you get there one day?" he said.

"Really?" asked Jack, who couldn't
believe his luck. Wait until Max hears
about this one, he thought.

Realizing it was time to go, Jack shook hands with Mr. Panini and said goodbye. He made his way over to the grandstand and found the seat where he had arrived. Since all the spectators had left by now, it was a perfect time and place for Jack to disappear. Punching a few buttons on his Watch Phone, he yelled, "Off to England!"

Within moments, Jack was transported home. When he arrived back in his bedroom, *Fast Cars* magazine was still in his hands. He turned back to page eighty-two and for the next twenty minutes read about his hero, Morgan Parks. Then he drifted off to sleep with a big grin on his face.

Find out more about
Secret Agent Jack Stalwart at

Great games, puzzles,
free downloads,
activities, competitions
and much more!

SECRET AGENT NOTES

SECRET AGENT NOTES

SECRET AGENT NOTES

SECRET AGENT NOTES

SECRET-AGENT NOTES

SECRET-AGENT NOTES

SECRET-AGENT NOTES

SECRET-AGENT NOTES

SECRET-AGENT NOTES

SECRET-AGENT NOTES

About the Author

Elizabeth Singer Hunt is originally from Louisiana, and now lives in California. Inspired by her love of travel, she created the Jack Stalwart series for her children.